A PAPI GOT ME

JADA

JUST BAE

ISBN: 9781925988406

CONTENTS

1
———

*J*ada pulled on the ropes binding her to the bed reveling in the erotic bondage as her boyfriend, Carlos was fucking the shit out of her. She was spread eagle on her back with a pillow under her ass, grounding and raising her pussy. This was the way Jada had hoped to spend her birthday; a perfect day to turn eighteen. She had been singing happy birthday in her mind as Carlos was hitting her walls left and right. Carlos was her neighborhood's bad boy; a Polo jacket-wearing Dominican who Jada's mother said was a rebel without a cause.

Jada loved the way he tied her, spanked her, and honestly, loved the way he fucked. Jada liked it rough, and he would tear it up brutally. She felt her climax approaching, and decided to let go. It was a nasty feeling she was enjoying. Jada grinned wickedly as she said something she'd never did before. "Fuck me harder, Carlos."

Carlos was on top; his dark curly hair hanging, a seashell necklace around his neck along with the five o-clock shadow of a man who hadn't shaven today. His eyes were closed when he said, "Brianna, you love Papi's dick, don't you?"

Jada paused. Chills started running through her as she tried processing what just happened. Brianna was her best friend.

Did this nigga really just say her best friend?
"What?"

Jada hoped she hadn't heard him correctly. Carlos opened his eyes, and what was written on his face was clear. He got caught and slowly stopped thrusting while Jada's mouth was hanging wide open.

"Oh no, you didn't."

This could not have happened, not today, not her birthday. Jada was betrayed by the two closest people she knew; her boyfriend and her bestie.

"Let me go now," Jada said beginning to tear up.

Carlos didn't move.

"Carlos, get this shit off of me now." Tears began running heavily from the corners of Jada's eyes.

Again, Carlos just stared. Then, he began going again. "Mommy, I fucked that mamasita but we're good right?"

"Carlos, stop. Stop right now. No! Carlos! No," screamed Jada, pulling on the ropes.

Carlos continued fucking her; pounding while Jada was twisting and turning trying to get free. When he was about to cum, Jada felt it. Moments later, Carlos came causing Jada to yell, "No." He then stood up putting on his pants.

"Somehow, this turned out to be a good day, Mami," said Carlos as he untied Jada. "Mami, you go to go. My mama is coming over."

"Fuck you!"

Jada sat on the bed for a minute crying. Then, she went into the bathroom and tried washing his cum out of her. Dressing quickly, Jada threw on her t-shirt, jammed her bra into her purse and laced up her shoes. She glanced around making sure she did not leave anything behind. Jada saw the Xbox One Carlos so much cherished. She grabbed and threw it out the window. It fell three stories to the parking lot of the apartment building.

"What the fuck, mommy?" Carlos came bursting in as Jada tried to run. He grabbed her, looked at the window, and started cursing. Jada kneed him in the balls but not before he slapped her. Jada felt her lip tear, tasting blood.

"I'm so done with you. Fuck you!"

Carlos was on the ground, holding his nuts. Jada

ran out of the apartment, taking the stairs, two and three at a time.

"Come back, Mami. I'm sorry!" shouted Carlos from the window. Jada didn't look up; her lip was swollen, but her heart was hurting more.

Jada got into her Honda and drove off. She didn't know where she was going, barely able to see through her tears. Her hands were shaking and her lip was bleeding. Minutes later, she was outside her home, double-parked barely inches from her brother's car. Jada wanted her mother now. She left the car door open, the engine running, and headlights flashing. She lunged for the front door and opened it finding her Dad and brother Shawn in the living room watching basketball.

"Hey! Birthday girl!" yelled Dad.

Jada didn't answer, walking by, searching for her mother. Her legs were hurting, as she went up the steps and found her mother in her bedroom, watching Scandal.

Mom looked up at her, and jumped to her feet. "What happened to you, baby?"

Jada threw her arms around her mother, holding on.

"Mom, I—I."

Dad and Shawn came upstairs and Mom said, "You two go back downstairs. Leave us, this is girl stuff."

Jada held on tightly, drowning in a sea of emotion and betrayal. Her face was on her mother's shoulder while she told everything. Much to Jada's surprise, her mother said, "I told you so, sweetheart."

"But, mom!"

"No butts. It's a tough way to grow up Jada, but you'll be fine."

"Mom, he did this to me." Jada showed her bruised lip.

"What did you do to him?"

"Kick him in the balls."

"Well, that's the least he deserved. Remember what goes around, comes around."

"Yeah, mom."

"God don't like ugly!"

Mom gave Jada an oatmeal bath, and had Jada wash carefully and then put her to bed."

"We will keep this between us. I don't want your father and brother to kill that boy."

"Ok, mom."

"Good night."

2

Jada graduated high school a few weeks later. As she prepared to come to Georgia for college, she found that Brianna was pregnant, and there was no doubt to who the father was. Jada had the satisfaction; small one of watching her former best friend go from prom to welfare queen.

She moved in with her aunt in Savannah, and started college at Savannah State. After two years of studying, Jada still had no direction in her life, so she just didn't sign up for the third. She started working and after bouncing around from job to job, before finally landing as a legal secretary for a law firm. Ten months of working for a bitchy boss lady, Jada had got fired for being late too often. Luckily, she found another one quickly as an assistant for a Dominican man who owned one of the largest book publishers in the area.

"This job is easy, Mami! Just make sure you submit the invoices on time and some other little things with Mr. Javier Sosa, our best client, but it's not too hard," the owner, Omar Rosario told Jada at the interview.

"Thanks, Mr. Omar. You can count on me. You've hired the right person."

Jada worked twenty hours a week, sometimes more, sometimes less, and was the lead assistant to Javier Sosa, the famous romance writer. She had been working now for a month and loved her job. She even had a little crush on Javier minutes after meeting him. Her attempts to make subtle passes at him had all been returned. Javier never followed up on Jada's verbal wordplay. Occasionally, he would stand close to Jada, leaning over her to read something or explain the way he wanted to see something done. It would cause Jada's insides to melt, and her heart would ache for the rest of the day when he would place his arm around her. Javier was in his twenties, single and cute causing Jada to wonder why he chose Savannah as home instead of Miami. Yet, Jada was convinced the key to finding out who her new boss was, was in the basement of his shop. It had to be, as there was no reason for a deadbolt to be on the door otherwise.

For his mailings, there was a stack of publicity photographs and software that would sign them in Javier's handwriting with whatever message Jada thought was appropriate. She handled all of Javier's daily stuff so he could focus on writing. His romances sold fairly well and were a bit popular. However, Javier would sometimes disappear twice a month or so, without telling Jada where he was going. Jada was instructed not to call his cell phone, and in case of an emergency, only send a text. Mr. Omar explained in her hiring package that the emergency had to be extreme. Yet, Jada went along only wondering about the deadbolt on the door in the other room.

Two weeks later, Javier had returned from one of his reclusive weekend business trips, a few days late and Jada felt insulted. As his personal assistant, she felt she was supposed to be in the loop about everything. Jada had made her point before, and during that discussion, she pointed out how Javier was too valuable to disappear like that, and needed to trust her. His reply stunned her.

"Jada, I don't think you're really in the position to

chastise me, just in case you had forgotten who the boss is."

"Sorry, Mr. Javier. It won't happen again."

"No, problema. By the way, since you are so curious to find out more about me, I've written a few mysteries which I think you'll find fascinating."

"Why you think I'm checking up on you?"

"Let's just say I know. Here are three of my mysteries. If you have time, go through them. You'll discover what you might or might not be looking for?" Javier giggled as he passed them to Jada.

"What's this some game, you're playing?"

"Just check them out. I have a business affair later this afternoon. Thanks for your help, Jada and help yourself to the donuts in the kitchen."

"Ok—well. Have a good trip."

Later that afternoon, Jada had skimmed through all the texts in the books Javier left. "It has to be a clue, it just has to be," she told herself. There were other clues that said a key had to be here. In the second book, the investigator was looking to enter a house, and told his partner "When you're trying to get into a locked house, look close by the door for a hidden key. They found a bunch of them, but didn't know which one unlocked the door?"

Jada stopped by the shop on the weekend which normally was her days off to snoop around. She was in the library across the hall from the basement door looking around for the key, feeling that it had to be hidden nearby. She looked behind the bookshelves she could reach behind and nothing. Perhaps it was behind one of the books, but there had to be at least three thousand. Some old, some new, arranged only Javier. Which book would he have hidden it behind? Jada started scanning titles for some differences that leaped out at her as significant. She followed the books from the left side of the door, and after covering half the left side of the wall, gave up. It was getting too far from the door. Going back to the door, she started on the right side looking over the titles again. Maybe something would leap out and grabbed her, however, Jada found nothing. It was almost eleven at night on a Saturday. Jada rather had been doing something else and decided it was time to go.

Monday afternoon, Jada was at her desk, nibbling on a chef's salad, and printing out the last of Javier's invoices. Minutes earlier, Jada had wrapped an order to place with for more business cards. She put her computer to sleep, and headed for the front door, slinging her purse over her left shoulder. As Jada passed the library, she stepped inside, wondering what she had missed. She walked around one last time, waiting for something to wave at her and scream, "Is it me, or I'm the next clue?" Stopping after steps, Jada turned slightly to her left looking at a shelf. One book didn't fit. The others were brown and this one was pinkish. Squatting down Jada looked at the title, "A Shaikh Got Me: Rachel by Just Bae" was typed on the spine.

"What in the world is this man reading? What he know about that?"

Jada pulled the book partially out and looked behind it. "No key. Damn well it was worth a shot." Headed for the door again. Jada put it out of her mind. She remembered reading that book a few months ago. Her copy was preordered but arrived right before she came to Savannah, The story itself was a hot and steamy novella. Jada stopped just short of the front door remembering her book had been titled "A Sheikh Got Me: Rachel not A Shaikh with an "A" in the word "Shaikh."

"Shit!" yelled Jada turning and dropping her purse. She pulled the book from the shelf and opened it. Inside was, a table of contents, and Jada felt the rush of satisfaction. She started flipping through the book, but for some reason, some pages were wedged together. As Jada separated the wedged pages, a ring with two keys fell out on the ground.

"Papi's a damn freak!"

Jada's eyes gleamed as she took the keys, laying the book aside on the table and walked across the hall. She smiled knowing this was the key to the door; the key to the mystery she had been seeking. Jada unlocked the deadbolt, and then the handle lock turned easily. Jada reached the bottom of the stairs to the darkened basement and a sensor on the door beeped. Meanwhile, Javier's cell phone had vibrated from the door's notification.

Jada found the switch at the bottom of the stairs, turned the lights on, stood stunned, looking at what looked like a sex dungeon. There were cages, a leather topped table, chains, whips, creams, and an incredible assortment of sex toys. Jada stepped around, looking at everything, shocked at what she saw.

"Oh my God!"

There were black chairs that had bindings built in, while more bindings, both leather, and steel hanging from the walls. Nude art hung on all sides, and each had a similar motif; a woman bound with each picture displaying different bondage positions. Jada felt a small thrill as she remembered when she had enjoyed such things with Carlos but not on this level. Her hand rested on a table as she looked at a picture of a woman stretched out on a large wooden X; bindings on her wrists and ankles while another strap around her waist. Jada's fingers danced across the chain, and for a moment she wondered what it would feel like to be stretched across this table, and have Javier on top of her prostrated and helpless. Her stomach tightened and her nipples stiffened slightly at the thought. Then she shook her head.

"No, no! Get it together, Jada."

Jada didn't want to do that anymore. She had that demon purged from her when Carlos had cheated on her. Never again would she be left helpless.

Meanwhile, Javier had been driving on I-16, out of Savannah; after a meeting with his broker, and then was off to a lunch invitation. He was headed west, and was ten minutes past the Statesboro exit when his phone buzzed. He growled, "This had better be an emergency. It's my weekend off. Damn it!" He reached for his phone and a couple button pushes later, was reading the message at sixty-five miles per hour. He read it twice to make sure he was, not mistaken. "I think this qualifies as such."

"Basement Door Breached," it read. Three words that told him everything. Jada was inside, and he needed to be there ASAP to calm her down before she ran screaming to the cops. Javier accelerated to seventy-five, and made an U-turn across the median, and accelerated back towards Savannah. He got off on the right exit, pushing past the speed limits on all the roads towards home while ignoring yellow lights that turned red as he reached the intersections. Fortunately, Javier's radar detector had remained silent, and no police were around.

Meanwhile, Jada was looking at the books on the shelves and picked up the one on the far right. Opening it, Jada found it had been published only a few months back. "The Family's Way of BDSM by Roja," and Jada couldn't believe it. *Was it possible that her boss had been writing two different types of books, mysteries, and smut?*

The next book to its left was "Short Stories by Roja" and Jada looked at it. It had been printed ten months ago and Jada had figured that Javier wrote this one also under the pen name of Roja.

"My boss is a damn freak! Oh my God! I'm telling—"

Minutes later, Jada heard Javier coming in. She could always sense his presence. It was just calling her. Jada had considered this evidence of a serious attraction between them, although unusual.

He was standing there by the steps and Jada was struck once again how good he looked. Dark hair hanging down to his shoulders, a tan sports coat over blue jeans and a polo shirt. The brown eyes that shone and cute cleft in his chin made his face gleam.

"I figured your little clues out."

"Yes, you did and now you know the secret of the basement. So, Ms. Sherlock Holmes, what do we do now?"

Jada felt a sudden rush of arousal and embarrassment. Swallowing hard, she replied, "Uh, what do you mean?"

"I meant, we should either talk about it, or you can run from the house screaming to the neighbors that Javier's a freak."

Jada almost smiled, but this was too serious for that kind of levity. Trying to change the subject, she asked "Did you write these books, too?"

"Yes, tell you what, bring them, I'll be in the office, and we can talk since you want to know," Javier said, turning to walk up the stairs.

Jada hesitated, then grabbed the books and followed him. When she entered, Javier was at his computer typing rapidly. He stopped and the printer started its cycle. Javier rose and took the printed sheet. He brought a pen over and handed both to Jada. "I think this should do nicely." She looked at the paper, reading it slowly. It was a letter of recommendation. It said her work was excellent and rated her extremely competent in all areas of office management. It severely regretted her loss and alluded to the difficulty of finding a similarly qualified assistant. Jada raised her head and said, "So, now I'm fired?"

"No, I assumed you would be thinking of quitting. II wanted you and any future employer to know how highly I thought of you."

Jada read the letter again. "I don't know. This is some creeping shit! Oops, I'm sorry."

"No problem, I understand. My story is fairly simple, Jada. I have been into BDSM since college, when I was first introduced. Obviously, it wouldn't do my public reputation any good to have that information out there, so I keep this on the down low, you know what I mean. The mysteries I write are good, and I enjoy writing them, but I love writing erotica. I love living the scenes out with others who share my tastes."

Jada looked at the books on the desk she had brought up. All had erotica-genre titles and short stories with a picture of a lady in handcuffs on the cover. All Jada could do was shake her head.

"Jada, I know you have flirted with me since you've started. I returned the favor but took no action because I need more than someone to fuck in my life. I need a submissive woman. The vanilla relationships are not satisfying to me anymore. After a few dates, I don't bother to call, because I'm bored."

"So you played along but didn't follow up because you didn't know if I was—?"

"Oh, don't get me wrong. I want you. I want to wine, dine and then bind you."

Jada shuddered slightly; partly from fear, partly from a rush of desire that began flooding her insides. Her throat was suddenly tight but she managed to get out, "I'm not in high school anymore."

Then Jada recalled that rainy afternoon when the power had went out at her place. Carlos had called and took her to his. They'd been fucking for almost an half an hour when Carlos first pulled out the handcuffs.

"So, let me make us some coffee. I think we got some things to talk about," said Jada.

3

———

ada had been speaking for almost thirty minutes nonstop, now feeling a little open. She was moved by Javier's stories about his former lovers, so she told him about Carlos, and her eighteenth birthday rendezvous.

"You told me about you, Jada, and I waited only now to tell you about me. I hate to say but you'll never grow out of being submissive. You'll never leave the feeling behind. Just had a bad experience, and I swear that wouldn't happen with me. However, I wanted to make sure your eyes were open. I wanted to let you know before we went out that submission is a biggie," said Javier. "I guess you can call it my fantasy. Now, you know, you decide what's our next move."

Javier stepped forward, and ran a single gentle hand down Jada's cheek. "I feel the same way you do,

Jada, I really like you. I look forward to seeing you every day, and feel my heart sparkle when I hear you. However, I know I won't be satisfied until I bind and pleasure you the way I think you still want deep down inside."

Jada listened, feeling an electric jolt run from her cheek electrifying her inners. She was happy, but angry Javier's love came with conditions. "So you can't fuck with me unless you get me all tied up"

"No, not exactly. You see I want you, but I want more of me that you would receive. I want your mind, body, soul, and heart. I want you, and offer all of me in return. I want your submission, with appropriate safeguards."

"Javier, I still don't understand. You want all of me, but you want more than that? What more is there?"

"There's so much more you wouldn't believe me if I told you. Some are in those books, while they are fiction, the scenes and emotions are real. There's another book I would like you to read as well. I'll go get it."

Javier left the room and Jada sat wondering what the fuck just happened.

Javier returned a minute later. "This is an autobiography of a full-time submissive. I think you'll find it interesting, and perhaps enlightening."

Jada sat looking at the books and thought what in the world is this guy into. "Javier, couldn't we try dating first? It's worked for generations, you know? " Jada tried smiling but couldn't. "You could always take me to a bar and get me drunk. Hey, you might get lucky."

"As for that, I want you mind, body, heart, and soul, which means I can't take advantage of you while you're intoxicated. Jada, the dating routine has worked to an extent but people in relationships often hide their feelings and desires."

"I don't want you holding anything back from me. I want you, without reservation. Your parents have a good marriage, but I bet if you ask your mom something personal about your father, she'll hold things back. I want more intimacy than what's allowed by that type of relationship." Javier said returning to his desk. He turned on the computer and began typing. The printer chimed again and several sheets came out.

"I want you to take some time to think about this. Read that and consider what you want. I have five copies." Javier took the papers and signed them one at a time, leaving the date and the signee's signature blank. "Anytime you're ready." He gave Jada the papers and said "Jada, please think about this. Don't let your fear and bad experience chase you away from a source of great pleasure and reward."

"Reward? I don't understand how this is rewarding. It sounds like a freak show."

"The reward is a sense of fulfillment, once you surrender."

Jada watched him leave the room and realized she was also dismissed. She didn't like the easy way he came at her. Jada's anger bubbled and she called after him. "When do you want me to tell you no?"

Javier stopped in the doorway. "I want whatever answer when you are truly ready to give it. In the meantime, take a few days off. Don't worry, you'll still get paid."

Javier walked out and Jada sat for a minute before gathering up the books. She walked to the front hall, got her purse, and left wondering if she'd ever return.

As she drove home, Jada wrestled with what just happened. The secret of the basement, but she still had more questions. What exactly did Javier want? Did he expect a black woman to become submissive?

She got home just before three, and walked upstairs with his books packed into her oversized purse. Jada had become frugal in her expenses, in an effort to save money. So far in her young adult life, nothing had worked out the way she hoped yet. Now this was taking an unexpected turn, and would probably make her even more jaded.

Jada considered reading one of the books at least. She was hooked by the storyline before she had turned the fifth page. It was well written, and Jada could relate with the characters. She could see the similarities in style and language and recognized it was Javier's. She finished the book close to 11 pm skipping dinner. Jada got up and made something quick to eat. She fell asleep minutes later.

Jada woke at ten in the morning, feeling refreshed but confused. The book she read was one of the most erotic stories ever. Love and obedience were intertwined throughout its plot. Worse, she had dreamed that Javier was doing those things to her; tormenting her, teasing her, and giving her those powerful orgasms. Jada remembered one scene from her dream, where she was bound, and Javier was lightly striking her with nipple clamps bouncing at every strike. She felt her nipples contract thinking about it, and her pussy started contracting.

"No, I'm not like that. Black women don't do this crazy shit," Jada nearly shouted in her empty apartment.

The ending of the story was kind of heartbreaking but the sexual content was the most real she's read. It made her recall all the cumming sessions she had with

Carlos. Orgasms that were mind-shattering especially when he had her handcuffed.

After breakfast, Jada started the autobiography of the submissive. Jada read the first chapter and set it down thinking it might possess her. It was way too extreme as it kept referring to the woman as a man's slave. Jada decided she didn't need to read further acknowledging that it might be true, sort of, but no way she could be this.

"I have got to get out of here for a while and get some fresh air."

4

Dressing quickly, Jada grabbed a few things and shoved them into her duffle bag, The vacation that Javier had recommended was fine with Jada especially after what she just read.

She left the books behind, not wanting them near her, afraid of the effect they would have on her. She tossed her bag in the backseat of her Honda and left Savannah heading west on I-16, for Macon, to her best friend, Britney.

Britney and Jada met in high school, and had been close ever since Jada started seeing Carlos. Jada would share her secrets with her and Britney would, too.

Jada called to make sure it was all good as she drove west on I-16.

"Hey, Brit. I'm coming down to check you out."

"What girl! You coming to Macon?

"Yeah, I'll be there in a few hours. I got a few days off. It's boring as fuck out here."

"Ok, hit me up when you're outside."

"Ok."

What happens if Britney doesn't tell you it's crazy to consider it. That thought wouldn't enter Jada's mind as she drove west.

Once Jada arrived, she played with the kids for a while, just enjoying getting away from everything for now. After dinner, Britney's husband Jay and the kids were watching TV when Britney and Jada walked over to the park. Jada had some things to get off her chest. After filling her in on the details, Jada asked. "So what do I do, Brit? How can my boss possibly expect me to do some freak shit like this? I should call the cops."

"You can't be his fuck mate for the rest of your life, so ask him if he'll do it for a week or two, better yet, give it a month."

"A month? Wait a minute, why would I want to be a slut for a month, girl? Are you crazy?"

Britney rolled her eyes. "Jada, you don't get it. Do you?"

"Get what? That this Papi wants me to be his little fuck slave?"

Britney looked at Jada confused. "Jada, two weeks

ago, you said you would do anything to have the guy. Now you know who he is, are you willing to be true to him?"

"I'm not for this shit," Jada spoke too fast, and both knew it.

"Jada, the only way you can have that rich Papi is on his terms. Remember something you told me about the times you had with Carlos. You said he ruined something you really enjoyed, and when I asked what, you said you loved being tied up and helpless. You said it made you feel good being that way."

"That asshole ruined it for me."

Jada started walking slowly again. "Jada, it's up to you. It's time to start eating boo. For the last few years, I've watched you go through the motions; going from this nigga to the next. You locked yourself away, until those dudes got close, and then you run. You ran from Atlanta to Savannah then ran away from college, and now your want to run from a rich Papi because he demands you give him some pussy."

"So, wait a minute! You're telling me to do it?"

"Jada, do you like him?"

"Yeah, he's kinda cute. You know I do."

"Jada, he told you he wants your heart, not just whatever you feel safe giving him. So do you believe him?"

"Yeah, I guess."

"Can you walk away? You know that's why he gave

you the reference letters. He knows it too, boo. If you say no, you can't go back."

"I don't know, Brit. I just don't know." Jada answered after walking a few paces. "I thought you'd tell me to be safe and not to do this. I didn't expect you to tell me to jump into deep shit."

"You wanted my honest opinion. I can tell you don't do it, stay in your lane and stay broke."

"No, girl. I really do value your opinion. That's why I came. You know that."

"I know, I just wondered if you knew."

"Damn I opened Pandora's Box by going in that basement."

"You sure did!"

"So it's either do this or I have to quit my job. Brit, I like the guy. My heart aches whenever he goes off to the book tours on one of his weekend adventures." "Shit, I have trouble breathing when Rico is next to me."

"Jada, Carlos took advantage of you, and make no mistake, it wasn't cool. When you said no and he didn't stop, that's rape. Before that, you'd smile and have that look that made me envy you. You used to live it up and now you're just living. Maybe this is what's missing, your need for a good partner."

"I've been with guys since, Carlos."

"Yeah, you have, and then dumped them, Jada."

"It's not easy, Brit. Fucking and being submissive is

something completely different. Your helpless, and I used to think that was kinky and fun, but now it's too scary."

"Jada, how many fantasies have you had about Javier?"

Jada stopped and looked. "Shit, that dream I texted you about. I forgot all about that."

"That's right, which is why I can't understand why you frontin' girl. You dream all of the time, don't you?"

"Well, not all this, but yeah. I had one dream where I was bound by him." Jada said trying to minimize her words.

Britany could see her friend wasn't totally convinced but still had hope. However, there was one thing she could say, but she wasn't ready to talk about, and Jada obviously wasn't ready to listen.

Jada walked home with Britany and spent the night there. In the morning, she said kissed the kids goodbye and headed back to Savannah.

5

———

Getting back to Savannah, Jada decided first to see if Javier was at home. If he was, maybe they could talk this over. And maybe there was an alternative after all. Britany didn't have to be right, perhaps Javier would give in and act normal.

Javier was in his driveway, polishing his Harley. He liked riding it when he couldn't concentrate on writing.

"Hola, Javier, Como estas?" Jada said as she got out of her car.

"Bien, bien, Jada. Hablas espanol? Y tu?"

"OK, let's stop there. I think you asked and me too, right?"

"Si, senora."

"I'm good. So, you stayed in town this weekend, I see?"

"Yeah, I decided it wasn't worth the headache. I wouldn't be able to relax and enjoy myself wondering about what would happen next." Javier set the cloth down he was using to polish the chrome and looked at Jada. "I was so nervous wondering if the woman I'm falling for was going to leave me."

"Ok, enough of the bullshit, Papi. Why me?"

"What?"

Jada took a long look at him while Jada stood shaking her head.

"Anyway, yeah, I came here, hoping to see you. Hoping to talk to you about this little arrangement you wanna have."

Javier nodded slightly and said "If you want to go on a couple dates, we can, but I'm sure it would destroy anything we have. I'm afraid we would both feel unsatisfied and leave each other within days."

"Ok, so my girlfriend had a suggestion; one which I think is worth discussing. Would you consider trying this out for thirty days, and if we like it, we'll see, and if not, we're good?"

Javier seemed to consider Jada's proposition for a moment. "So you want to try this out for a month, you're saying, Mami?"

"Yeah, if you—"

"Then, I think that might work."

"My girl said you would, but I didn't think so. Can I ask why?"

"Jada, right now you're looking at this as a chore, and if I can't change your mind, that's all it will be even if you said "yes" unconditionally. If it's that, you'll leave my proposal quicker than a month."

Jada was puzzled by Javier's response but quickly changed subjects. "I was wondering, where do you go when you take off for those long-ass weekends?"

Javier rose. "Let me put the bike away, and then we can talk."

Jada followed Javier inside, carrying in some cleaning materials, after they put a few things in his garage. Once inside, Javier surprised Jada by not going to the office, instead of heading for his living room. Javier signalled for her to sit and then left the room. Once he returned, he put a disk inside the room's DVD player.

"There's a retreat, about halfway between Macon and Atlanta, sort of a ranch. It's a getaway for swingers. People who have a membership, go there to live their fantasies for a few days."

"So a club for freaks?"

"If that's what you want to call it." Javier snickered.

"There are all types of activities. There are lodges, entertainment and races."

"Races?" Jada asked confused.

"Pony boys and girls."

Jada was still confused.

Javier turned on the TV and started the DVD player. "This is last year's horse race."

Jada watched as women dressed in leather harnesses and bikinis were pulling what appeared to be carts. They walked past the camera, wearing head masks and waving to the crowd. The first race started and the girls raced around the track once; each having a man jockey fucking her in the cart as it pulled off. Jada sat in shock watching it with her mouth open in disbelief. She put her hand on her head and sank back further. The first race ended and the winner stripped naked while her name was announced. There were cheers as the remaining participants were presented one by one. As their names were called, they stripped and then jumped in the crowds of men doing all types of sexual acts.

"Oh my God! This can't be happening."

"It does. This weekend I was going to watch a training, to see who has the best chance to win on the big day. This year, it's in New York and next year's will be here in Georgia."

"What do you pay to see the girls humiliated like that?"

"Nothing, they aren't humiliated. They are proud to be in this event and make good money, believe me."

Jada blinked and watched the second race, more

girls, same type of outlandish outfits. A black woman won, and Jada gaped at the outfit she was wearing. Her breasts were bared in black leather. She had a flog between her teeth as she stood in knee high boots with small heels. She looked between the camera while the announcer kneeled and licked her pussy. She held the man's head in place, watching him doing it, while the emotion on the woman's face showed satisfaction.

"That's Monica, and she's the favorite to win it all this year." Javier said. "This is her third year racing, last year she lost by an inch. Mistress Elizabeth has trained her differently, and it has helped Monica improve."

"Different, huh?"

"Yeah, really different."

Jada looked at Javier, shook her head again and then looked back at the screen.

The pony boys came next wearing crazier costumes and had rings around their dicks.

Jada put her hand on her mouth as she watched the men race while the women were deep throating them in the cart. They were all in prime shape and all Jada could do was shake her head. "You couldn't pay me a million dollars to do that."

"Everybody has a way of earning their livelihood. There are no rules except those we make for ourselves.

These performers choose to do this, and are free to leave anytime. We cheer them on and don't feel that they are doing anything wrong. They are only performers."

"So, no rules?" "Is that how you convince those people to humiliate themselves, by telling them there are no rules?"

"Jada, if we made rules, they won't be violated. If you don't want to do it, don't do so. No one in that video was forced. There wasn't any close ups of anyone who didn't agree both beforehand, and again after the video was produced. Each person signed a waiver to approve each scene."

"I didn't mean anything like you just said. Where are people's morals? This is so extreme."

"Jada, you asked what I do on the weekends. I go away, among other things and watch those talented people. I hold them in great esteem." Javier said punching the remote button turning the TV off. He rose, ejected the disk, and left the room.

Jada sat thinking if this was okay for some form of cheap underground entertainment, God knows what goes on outside the camera.

The doorbell rang and Javier answered it. Jada rose and Javier glanced back at her while opening the door.

"Doug, I was hoping to see you, glad you could stop by," Javier said. "This is my assistant, Jada."

Doug came in and shook Jada's hand. "So you're Jada? It's a pleasure to finally meet you."

Jada looked towards Javier for an explanation and after moments of silence said, "Uh, thanks, nice to meet you, too, Doug."

"Jada was just about to leave. Doug, you know where the office is, please help yourself. The coffee's hot."

Jada was being dismissed again, and didn't like it. She waited until Doug was down the hall. "Javier, I was hoping we could – you know – talk about this little freak thing a bit more. This is really hard to digest."

Javier shook his head. "I think we have spoken enough for today. You're still undecided. If it makes you feel better, you won't be fired. If you never work for the next five years, and never come back, your direct deposits will continue to posted. Think about it, Jada. I have some business to attend to."

"And that's what you got to say?"

"Yes, for now. Good afternoon."

Jada walked out, and heard the door close behind her. She got in her car, and drove home. She wasn't even in the apartment for ten minutes before she was calling Britany telling her the freaky shit this dude just showed her.

6

"Jada, when are you going to pull your head out of your ass?"

Jada got angry. It seems like her best friend was pushing her in a direction she didn't want to go. "Britany, I'm not a damn freak. You know I'm not. You aren't like that so why are you pushing me to do it?" Jada slammed the phone and ignored it when it rang a minute later.

Jada cooked some dinner and was fuming while watching TV when there was a knock on the door. She glanced over at the clock and wondered who would be knocking at ten at night. Glancing through the peep hole, she saw Britany. When she opened the door, she gasped seeing that her best friend brought Jada's Mom, Carol with her, too.

"Mom, Britany, what are you doing here?"

Britany pushed her back and said, "First, let me say you don't hang up on me, girl. Second, we came to save you from your black ass."

Jada watched her mom come inside pulling her luggage.

"We're here for the next few days. I'm concerned that you might be back to where you while you were with crazy Carlos. My daughter ain't gonna make another mistake."

Jada looked between Britany and her mother. "I don't need nobody to protect me. I'm okay."

Britany was looking at the phone and said, "Do you have Javier's number? We need to let him know that you won't be in to work for the next day or two."

"What? No, you didn't, girl. Oh my God!"

"Oh! Yes, I did. Me and Mom are tight and she needs to be in on this one."

Jada was caught off-guard and was trying to get her mind onto the scene that was unfolding in her living room. "Mom, tell me again, why are you here?"

"Britany called telling me how confused you are, and after you hung up on her, I dropped everything, drove to her place, and we came right away."

"Carol, perhaps Jada should know everything. You

know how we became BFFs. All the little things," said Britany.

Jada looked at them confused. "What little things, BFFs, how long, and what the hell is going on?"

"We both are down with the freaky-freaky, baby. Me and your girl were talking one day in the kitchen while you were upstairs getting dressed and some books came up. From there, we've been giving book recommendations, going to conferences, and etc. Of course, we can't let the guys in on our little secret?" said Jada's mom.

Britany proceeded, "We've been talking for years, and found we had some things in common, for example, we both enjoy being tied up, bound and submissive. We both enjoy reading erotica, especially good black men in bed."

Carol jumped in. "So after you hung up on Britany, she called and filled me in. I decided it was time to come out of the closet (so to speak) and talk to you about some girl stuff."

Jada sat down on the couch and said, "I need a drink."

Britany turned towards the kitchen and said "God yes, do you have some rum?"

"Yeah, there's some and coke in there."

"Shit, it's Sunday. I went to church today. Lord forgive me." Britany grabbed the bottle and took three glasses to the living room and sat.

Jada held her glass and while Carol and Britany clinked cheers.

"Let me get this straight, my best friend, and my mother, both appreciate this freaky shit. Now that alone is enough to send me to a mental institution. Now, they're here to convince me that I do it?" said Jada.

Carol turned towards her and said "Jada, it's your fault I like it, baby."

Jada looked shocked. "My fault, Mom? What the fuck?"

"Don't curse, baby! The Lord will strike us down."

"Let me continue. You see while you were doing your little thing with Carlos, mommy came and cleaned up your room. I saw your little outfits, hand-cuffs and etc. I couldn't talk to Dad about it. It just happened that Britany and I were talking one day and we touched on the topic. She told me about some books to read and the stories I read made me passion-ate. I finally worked up enough courage to explain to your father what I wanted, and we started doing it occasionally."

Jada emptied her glass and poured more rum. "I am going to need an army of shrinks. My own mother is sitting here telling me about her sex life with my father."

Britany laughed and said, "Well, my story is similar, I had always thoughts of being kinky. I read a couple of books in my junior year in high school, and well, my husband and I tried it one night. Now, once a month or so, we send the kids over to a friend's house and I play slave girl to him."

Jada slid off the couch. "Am I the only normal person here?"

Carol came and sat next to her daughter. She put her arms around her. "You had a bad experience with Carlos, and it wasn't your fault. He betrayed, and took advantage of you." Britany reached out and placed her hand on Jada's shoulder. Carol continued, "Since that day, you haven't been the daughter I've known. I have watched you dabble here and there. You haven't stuck with anything, just floating around. You went from the top of your class with the whole world at your feet to someone who hides in this tiny ass apartment and runs anytime things start getting hectic."

Jada felt tears in her eyes. "Mom I can't—I can't do this."

Britany interjected, "You can, and you have to, Jada. This could be a chance of a lifetime. I'm afraid if you don't, you may never get another."

They stayed up most of the night talking. At about dawn, everyone slept scattered about the apartment. Jada was on the floor, her mother on the couch, and

Britany in Jada's room. At noon, Jada woke Britany when going to the bathroom. Carol and Britany knew it would take some time to get Jada right.

Later in the day, Carol and Britany talked everything through with Jada while out and about. Jada, Carol, and Britany took turns reading the books by Javier, and would read aloud the "good parts" to one another; oooing and ahh-ing.

By Tuesday morning, the healing had truly begun, and by Thursday, Britany said she was ready. Jada was convinced she could be submissive and do what was asked.

"Jada, you're all better now, we've done what we could. Javier's waiting for you," said Britany.

Carol said "I couldn't agree more. My daughter is back, and it's about damn time."

Jada smiled at her best friend and mother. "Thanks, I really appreciate it. Is there anything I can do for you?"

Britany looked at Carol and smiled wickedly. "Do you think you could get us some autographed copies of Javier's books?"

Jada nodded and said "I'll get on that for you. Five autographed mysteries coming right up."

Carol shook her head and said, "The other books, Jada, we've been reading this week. They are truly something erotic."

Jada rolled her eyes. "Mom, that might be harder,

but I'll see what I can do." Jada remembered seeing a few copies downstairs in a box when she had grabbed the five to follow Javier upstairs. "Will you come with me to meet him?"

Britany and Carol exchanged glances and agreed.

They decided it made sense to take two cars so that Carol and Britany could leave from Javier's and head straight home. Jada parked where she always did. They walked to the house, and Jada found the door unlocked and motioned the others to come in. "Javier, I have some people I'd like you to meet if it's OK."

Javier stepped out of the office and walked to the front. "Certainly Jada and who are these lovely ladies?"

Jada introduced her mother and Britany. "They'd like some autographed books, and have been here working to help me understand more about my submission issues."

Javier was caught off guard. "Really, and how did it go?"

Jada said "Very well, I believe we can begin later today, my love."

Javier looked at Jada, and saw the twinkle in her eyes.

"Surely, would you do me the honor of getting two complete sets? Bring them to the office and I'll be happy to sign them."

Jada nodded. "Yes sir. Britany, Mom, please go with Javier and I'll join you shortly."

Javier took the ladies to his office, and showed them the desk that Jada worked at. "This room used to be my mother's favorite room, but I turned it to my little office. I use the dry boards along that wall to map out the stories, as you can see, I'm working on a mystery now. The majority of it is already been written, and now I'm working on putting in the clues. That's the hard part, figuring out how to solve the crimes you've created."

"Javier, Jada let us read some of the other books you have written. I mean the nasty ones. I thought they were great," said Britany.

Javier looked at Britany. "Thank you, it's always nice to have your work applauded."

Jada came in the office with two boxes, and Javier's eyebrows raised. Obviously, there were more than the five books he had told her.

"Great, Jada. Thanks a lot!" Javier said taking the boxes and going over to his desk. A quick glance showed there were his sets of erotica novels. "While you are certainly welcome to the books ladies, I'll admit that I've never signed these works before. Would you prefer that I sign them "Sierra" or my own name?"

Britany and Carol looked at each other and shrugged. Then, Britany said, "I think we'll leave that up to you. I understand the need to keep these little things in the closet, or dungeon if you like."

Javier glanced at Jada. "It looks as you have an

interesting story to tell me later, amor." Then, he began signing, and within minutes, Javier handed them their copies.

———

They chatted for about fifteen minutes, and then Britany and Carol headed out.

Closing the door after watching them drive away, Jada turned to start the next facet of her life. Javier and Jada returned to the office and Javier turned facing Jada. "How are you feeling now, amor?"

Jada looked at Javier for a moment, and then slowly dropped to her knees before him. There was a short silence before Jada spoke. "Command as you wish."

With a crotch that hardened noticeably, Javier replied, "I see you're ready. Would you like to discuss limits and choose your safe word?"

"Papi, I'm going to assume that you already have a safe word, and as for limits, I don't know enough yet to set any."

"Rise, Jada."

Jada kissed his crotch and rose to her feet. Javier looked into her eyes and saw them sparkling. "Where did you learn that?"

"Your books, one scene described this position, and I figured I should do it. I couldn't practice with my best friend and mom around," Jada said smiling but still puzzled that she was actually being this way.

"So what do I call you? Master, Daddy, Javier, Papi?"

"In public, you can refer to me as Master, that will be your term of honor to me. For now, Javier is appropriate, since we haven't had a collar ceremony. In the circle I run, the partners are called doms and subs if they are not collared. If they are, then they're masters and slaves. Is this clear?"

"Not really, what's a collaring ceremony. Sounds like being a dog which is a little bit too much for me. I don't remember that from the books."

"It's a domination ceremony. It's kinda hard to explain. Just say you will be taking me as your master and forsaking others without my permission. Basically, I'm taking you as my slave by placing you first in my life and heart."

"Sounds good."

Javier walked behind her and whispered into Jada's ear. "Tell me about your week; this is an amazing change in you."

"Papi, my mom and best friend helped me rid the last of my doubts. They also helped me realize what matters. More importantly, they got me to understand my life has been empty, because I walked away from being submissive. I spent years pretending I was something I wasn't, and discontented.

Javier stood above Jada. "They brought me a woman I knew existed inside you. The woman I have loved since she showed up looking for a job. I owe them more than a few books." He drew in a deep breath and leaned forward kissing Jada gently and backing away. "Go downstairs and wait for me."

Jada left the room and Javier went to lock the front door. He forced himself to remain calm. Taking a deep breath, he headed down to the basement. He arrived at the bottom step, he found Jada bowing, waiting. Javier felt his dick becoming harder, and fought down the surging urge to take her right then. Javier swallowed, struggling to stay focus.

"Rise Jada, come with me." Javier walked to the table and stopped. Jada stood beside him.

"All the connections in this room have been changed out. Each one has a quick release attached now." He showed the binding to Jada. "When you are in one of them, all you have to do to escape the binding is tug the small cord here and the binding breaks loose from the chains." He tugged the rope and a lever moved, and the binding came loose from the chain.

Jada smiled; he understood her fears because of her bad experience with her ex-boyfriend.

"Thank you, Papi."

"No worries, my love."

Javier next took her to a modified cross made from a heavy chain. It had four chains coming diagonally from the ceiling and floor. Then, it ended forming a large box that the victim would be outlined by. This alteration allowed a dom to work not only the front of the victim, but the back as well.

Javier kissed Jada again, this time more passionately. Then he stepped back before saying, "Take off your clothes."

Jada hesitated at first, but then slowly started to take off her blouse. She felt so sexy as she set her shirt aside. Next, she removed her breasts from her bra. Her pussy began to wet her panties. Licking her lips, she then removed her trainers and sweatpants. Jada stood before Javier in only panties, not knowing what to do next.

Javier came over and hugged her. Then, he whispered, "Very goodm Jada, that wasn't easy."

"Thank you, Papi."

Jada kissed him back, feeling her nipples harden. Javier lowered his head, kissing his way down her chest, reaching and holding her by the hips. He slid Jada's panties down, past her round ass, and then down her legs. Her fragrance filled the room; an intoxicating scent of heat. Javier then placed Jada's wrists and ankles into the bindings; her frame was spread before him. "My God, you are gorgeous, Jada."

Jada smiled and looked down. "Thank you, Papi."

Javier ran his hands over her neck, down to her breasts. Hefting them into his hands, he felt their weight, and ran his thumbs over her brown nipple. They hardened into their fully erection at Javier's touch. He then looked into Jada's eyes seeing her wet lips. Jada was panting as Javier kept playing with her nipples. He sucked them causing Jada to force her head back. She moved them onto his lips, causing her to moan.

Javier then kissed Jada on the neck and then began licking downward. The chains rattled as Jada tried moving her hands, to draw Javier in. He caressed her, stopping just short of her pubic hair. Javier then reached for the peacock feather on the wall, and began stroking Jada up and down; behind the knees, along the outside of her thighs, and under her breasts. He rubbed Jada's ass with the feather's edge, giving Jada goosebumps.

On the next pass, walking around, Javier picked up a suede flogger. Its subtle softness would only entice Jada even more. "This won't hurt, but I want you to breathe deeply." Jada nodded seeing the cord intertwined between Javier's fingers.

Javier began lightly flicking up and down; across Jada's breasts, down her middle, down her thighs, up her calves and the backs of her legs. He flogged Jada's back and buttocks a bit harder, telling her to breathe.

"Jada, keep breathing. This will release the endorphins, causing you to enter subspace."

"Oh, Papi."

Jada moaned, but her vision was blurring. Javier took some clips from the shelf and thumbed her nipples, perking them up. Placing one on the first, Jada let out a sigh of pain as the tiny clip pinched. Placing the second one on her other, Jada held it in.

"Relax yourself into the pain, my love."

Jada complied slowly, at first breathing slowly and then deeply. Her eyes were rolling in the back of her head and now she felt a sense of subspace.

"Oh, God." Jada felt intense sensation, but not painful. It was erogenous, arousing, and robust. Jada felt like she was actually flying.

Javier went back to flogging her softly. He put his hand over her vagina finding it heated and enlarged. It was ready for action; her pussy was creamy, sticky, wide, and so wet. Javier began to gently massage it. Jada moaned slightly and pushed herself out towards his hand. Javier flogged her a little harder as he slid his finger in. Jada moaned and her pussy muscles clamped down, holding him in. Jada was ready; ready for her first orgasm by her Papi.

Javier began to flick harder and rub her clit, and as his finger stroked, Jada cried in pleasure. Javier flogged her ass harder causing her redbone skin to redden. He flicked her clit rapidly and saw Jada tug on her bindings and saw her body tremble. Jada was so close right now.

Javier took her nipple clamps in one hand and released her left breast. He rubbed her clit harder and faster as the blood rushed back inside the nipple. Jada cried out in pain and pleasure as the second clamp was released. Her climax submerged her at that moment and she began making unintelligible sounds as she pulled on the chains. More cream came out of her pussy which covered Javier's hand. He continued flicking her clit, stirring it higher, and higher.

When Jada was done cumming, she hung limply from the chains as her legs were unable to support her weight. She was shaking; a little drooling was coming down from her lower lip. Jada breathed raggedly as Javier freed her ankles, and wrists. Javier carried her to the couch and placed her down. He then snuggled up with her and covered her with a blanket. Jada wrapped her arms around him.

"My—my that was surreal," stuttered Jada.

"The least we could acheive." Javier answered as he kissed her. "Now, that you know its power, you'll begin to reap its rewards."

Jada looked at Javier, leaned in and kissed. Her hand moved down to his dick finding it blocked by his pants. She fumbled with his belt before finally unbuckling it. There lied a pair of boxers between her and it. Jada pulled his dick out, and began jerking it. She felt heat inside; a heat that could be described as pure lust. Lust of her young pussy riding Papi's dick . She hadn't experienced this feeling even with Carlos.

"Javier, I want this dick now. No more of these little games."

Javier stood up and lowered his pants. As his dick cleared the boxers, it sprang up, hard and upright. Jada clutched it instantly and lowered her head inward. She moistened it; sucking and licking. Jada bobbed as her lips was the only thing making contact. After a few strokes, Javier pulled Jada's head up. Jada knew what time it was. She followed his lead and laid back on the couch. Javier mounted on top, placing his dick's head at Jada's pussy's hole and then slightly penetrated. Jada licked her lips and moaned. Javier slowly slid inside and Jada wondered if she could manage every inch. It filled her, and kept filling. Suddenly Jada felt full. Her hunger satiated for the moment, as Javier began to gently go in and out.

Jada put her arms around Javier and pull him into her. Her nails dug deep so desperate for the affection she had denied herself over the last two years. Javier was getting her there.

He lowered his head to her nipple, taking one in his mouth. He sucked and licked the areola while maintaining his stride. Jada had thrown her head back and had her hands grab his head. His actions on her nipples seemed to go straight to her pussy, making her more aroused, hotter, and brought her closer to cumming. Jada pulled Javier deeper into her.

Surprise struck then, and almost hurt as he was pounding. Jada felt at a lost for words, as she yelled out his name. Holding on, she tried her best to minimize her orgasm but couldn't.

"Oh! Papi, oh-no. Oooooooooo! I'm cumming, ahhhhhhh!"

Javier climbed off, and picked her up. Jada held on as he carried her to the leather table. Jada looked up at him with tears in her eyes trying to understand what was next. Javier laid her down and positioned himself between her legs.

Spreading, Jada reached to pull him back inside her. Javier positioned, and entered Jada in one full momentum. She felt her breath driven out of her as he did so. From this angle, Javier would achieve the highest penetration. Jada knew she couldn't take much more of this.

The wet sound of his dick sliding in and out her mixed with the moans, groans, and name-calling of both were satisfying. Jada cried out when she came again, and then gripped the edge of the table over her head as Javier continued to thrust into her like a mad man. Sweat was pouring from his body as his hands pawed her breasts; tugging, pinching, and gripping. Javier grumbled as his own cum started to ready. He gripped Jada's hips and drove himself inside with one final thrust.

Jada felt him about to cum and yelled when she felt his hot semen splash in her. Javier held her tight as he kept trying to cum deep inside. Jada smiled as he kept stroking feeling his warm cum all in her walls.

Javier came down slowly and looked at Jada. "So was this better than dinner and a movie, hmm?"

Jada smiled. "I think so, but I guess it would depend on what movie."

They embraced for a while and then showered. After they had a light lunch and Javier returned to his work on the storyboard for his latest mystery.

7

"*I* didn't see a board for the other books, where do you chart them?" Jada asked.

"I don't, I just let them flow. It doesn't really matter if something is out of order, or an item needs to be inserted. I can do that because erotica readers don't mind if the story isn't perfect. However, mystery readers demand perfection."

"I have a question, about the DVD you showed me, the races. Will you take me to one?"

Javier stopped looking at the board and turned, registering his own questions. "You want to go now?"

"Yeah, why not. You got me open. Better do it before I change my mind." Jada chuckled. "Are there any this weekend?"

"This weekend, there's only doing light training. The big one is in New York this year. I'm not sure you're ready for that crowd. There are some crazy-ass people there if you know what I mean."

"No, I don't know. Please explain?"

"Gothics, punk rockers and weirdos. They're a rowdy bunch."

" I get you now. Yeah! That ain't my thing." Jada snickered. "About this little submissive thing we got going on, how much of this will I need to know?"

"Basic positions at the minimum. Understanding of how to greet your dom, and how to greet a visiting one. How to behave in public, for example, you would be expected to kneel beside me when I'm seated. Walk on my right side, and wear a collar and leash to indicate you are my slave, and not being available for public or private sessions."

Jada looked pale, and said, "What the fuck's all that? Oops! I just lost my cool. Lord, forgive me but what in the world?"

"No problem, you're learning but there's that and more."

Jada swallowed and said, "Well, can we just not do the collar thing. I'll wear anything but I'm no dog?"

"There is some flexibility but let's talk about the attire. Leather is common, silks and satins are less. However, this is about posture and behavior more than a costume. For example, if I said collar position, you would need to know what to do."

"But in public? I don't know if I can go through with all this? I dig you and all, but I'm no dog."

"My dear, these are private events. No one knows except those who are members."

"Okay, then."

Jada tried to remember where she had read the collar thing. "This was in one of your books, wasn't it? The collar position?" She got off the chair and knelt before Javier; raising her hair off her neck. "Like this?"

Javier walked over and began adjusting her posture. "Pride, Jada, posture for a slave means she is proud to serve her dom."

"My greeting was okay, right?"

"It was pretty good for a beginner. If we practice the rest of the afternoon, I can probably teach you enough to get by. Then, we'll have lunch and go find you some outfits in Atlanta. This weekend will be light, less formal, and less of the expected submissive public stuff. More like a fun gathering. You'll still need to be deferential, but not as blatantly as you would on a normal weekend.

Jada smiled. "I'll work hard on this, and try not to embarrass you."

"It's not me who will be embarrassed."

Jada raised an eyebrow not knowing what Javier meant.

The rest of the afternoon was spent trying to get Jada to kneel properly, assume the correct positions and moving with grace. After a late lunch, they took a break and Javier told her about the ranch.

"Cell phones are checked at the gate, no cameras. The video I showed you was an exception and was announced months ahead. Privacy and trust are the golden rules," explained Javier.

"Among the members of this group is a member of Congress, a former Governor, television personalities, and rich and powerful personalities from as far as California. Hollywood actors and actresses. Don't stare at them. As a slave, you aren't supposed to look directly in the eye unless invited to do especially on working weekends. Even during the relaxed days, you shouldn't stare, but you can look at others more freely."

Jada tried absorbing all of this. This world of kinks was so much bigger than she had thought. "Cell phones checked at the gate, so that's why you're only allowed to verbally send messages?"

"Yes, the security tell the concierge and then he passes the message to the member. Cell phones are tagged with the members name, or pseudonym in the case of the known members."

"I'm surprised this place hasn't been featured on the news; a Dateline kind of thing."

"Not all that surprising considering that the

producers of most of those cable shows are members in good standing including the owners of the most major broadcasting companies."

Jada looked at Javier wondering if he was joking. Probably not she thought. "Anything else I need to do to keep me from looking like an ass?"

"We need to trim your pubic hairs, and shave but that can wait until morning. I'm considering trimming you a charming little heart."

"So, it's traditional to have your slave trimmed?"

"You'll see. I think you'll enjoy it. It makes the region more sensitive, and its activity becomes more erotic." Javier put his arm around Jada pulling her in. "My love, you'll see a world you won't believe."

Jada tried picturing what the full-fledged event would be like. "So, I'm supposed to be submissive while we're there, just not like how I am now?"

"Yes, after Friday, things will ease some. But Friday night, the expectations are a bit higher. It's a more stringent environment and the commotions are more. On Saturday, during the races or in this case preparations, the scenes are more relaxed, and subs often sit with their doms, and enjoy the entertainment."

"Ok, then. I see there's a lot to learn. Where's my notebook?"

"You'll get it. It just takes a little practice, amor."

"If it's more relaxed on Saturday, why not have a less stringent Friday?"

"Simply put, because we tend to use the stricter days to orient ourselves. Most have worked all week, and need Fridays to put us in the frame of mind. Some skip Friday nights, but I've always felt they set the tone for the days ahead."

Jada and Javier talked about what to expect at the ranch, the lodges, and other venues. It was almost too much to believe for Jada. After talking for another hour or so, they went upstairs to Javier's bedroom for the first time, and Javier started giving guidance. "Ready position, my slave."

Jada complied, kneeling as they had worked on earlier. She didn't look up at him but instead kept her eyes down. She knew this was a test, and if she wanted to go, she had to pass.

"Now, greet your dom," Javier commanded next.

Jada bowed deeply, and placing her hands on the ground touching his shoe with her forehead, and then her lips in turn. She returned to keeping her forehead on Javier's shoe, awaiting her next instruction.

"Am I doing this right?"

"Until you spoke," chuckled Javier. "Jada, the best way to enjoy this is to free your mind. Don't worry, don't overthink. Just go along with it. Let me do the thinking and worrying."

"Ok, Papi but don't kill me, okay?"

"Don't worry, my love."

"Ready position." Javier watched Jada as she

moved. She knelt with her knees about a foot apart; her hands on her knees, while her fingers joined and extended. Her back was straight, and bottom touched the heels.

"Greet another master," Javier said next. Jada rose and performed a similar movement to greet and the only difference was she didn't touch the shoe. She placed her forehead on the backs of her hands with her hands on the ground before the shoe and waited.

"Return."

Jada returned to the ready position.

"Not bad. Assume collar position."

Jada rose until her thighs were straight, kneeling. She placed her hands under her hair behind her neck, and raised her hair out of the way allowing access to her neck while keeping her head and eyes focused on the ground before her. She tried ignoring the heat from within, which seemed to radiate outwards from her stomach.

"Good Jada, really very good for your first day," said Javier. "Now, rise my love."

Jada stood and waited, as Javier moved around her and began undressing her. Soon, Jada was naked and Javier led her to his bed. He laid Jada down, kissing her and running his hands all over her. He played with Jada's nipples, and fondled the sensitive area underneath. Jada moaned as her desire increased. Javier kissed his way down, and then felt his tongue part her clit. Jada moaned again and gripped his head, holding him right there. Javier backed his mouth away slightly and said, "Hands behind your head."

Jada did what she told; having to intertwine her fingers to make sure she didn't move. As Jada heated up more, she was so relaxed. She accidentally put her hands down onto Javier's head again. Javier kissed his way back up.

"I can see we're going to have to restrain you. You're being naughty."

"Oh, daddy, no. Please don't," said Jada playfully.

She watched while Javier got the straps and bindings from under the bed. Apparently, they were already latched to the bed posts, and Jada soon found herself with her wrists bound to her ankles, and her legs spread open. Javier added bindings that ran from her elbows to her knees, and then secured her knees further by drawing them apart with straps secured to the bed.

Jada wiggled and held the strings that would release all the bindings in case of an emergency with a gentle tug. Javier went back to licking her pussy, bringing her quickly to the point of cumming. Then he backed away and licked her outer labia, probing her canal. Jada whimpered and felt the orgasm slightly go away, but Javier wasn't done yet. He kept bringing it back but it was taking forever. As Jada came close, Javier would ease away, making her arousal soar. Jada wanted to cum now was ready to beg for it.

"Please Javier, no more. Fuck me, Papi, please."

Javier smiled as he continued teasing her, bringing her up a little more into agonizing desperation. He took off his clothes, and his dick was hard as a rock waiting to strike.

Javier kissed his way up again, licking along Jada's thighs to her knees which seemed to frame her breasts. He positioned his dick at the entrance of her wet pussy, and gently entered. Jada came as he did, squirting. Her body shivered from the climax, and she kept on shaking as if it would never end. As Javier slid in and out, Jada just kept cumming. After a few minutes, her vibrations waned.

Jada could hardly see, as if she was in a sort of dream. She felt as limp as a wet noodle. Javier went in and out slowly, and Jada came out of her state. She pulled on her bindings, trapped, as Javier did as he deemed fit. She felt she was about to cum again, almost hoping that there was an end somewhere. Jada appeared to be going crazy, and didn't think she could take much more.

Javier bit down on her nipples causing a little pain. Jada cried out, breathed deeply, and then felt she was near subspace but not yet. Jada called out Javier's name as her pelvis bucked. Her pussy muscles contracted as sweat fell between her breasts. The last cum surprised her; it was quick but powerful. Her entire body strained against itself, and the bindings. This was it; her head was going to explode, and heart was going to give out. Jada was being fucked to death. Her pussy clamped down harder on Javier's dick, and he kept stroking in and out in a rhythm. He pushed her in areas that she suddenly realized were all wanting his dick's attention. Jada's head went back, knowing that she couldn't possibly endure another one.

Javier saw she was nearly drained, and smiled. He was about to cum. He reached down and began playing her clit. Jada opened her eyes wide and shook her head "no".

"Cum, Jada, Cum for me now." Javier started stroking while flicking her clit faster. Jada's eyes rolled back into her head. "Oh, daddy. Oh, daddy. Oh my God!" Javier trapped her clit under his thumb, and flicked it quickly. He saw Jada was there, and then she came but this time it destroyed her. This time she didn't whimper or make a small cry, she screamed out to the world. "Ohhhhhhhhhhhhhhhh!"

Once her convulsions subsided, Jada had tears in her eyes. Javier started picking up his own pace, hitting faster, and then faster. His balls tightened up and moments later, he came all inside of Jada. She grabbed Javier's buttocks and held him in, making sure he gave her all his nut. Javier was shaking and couldn't stop cumming.

Javier finished and Jada felt his dick going down. He laid down kissing her as his dick went limp two minutes later. He then got up and released the chains binding Jada and the leather cuffs. They cuddled for a bit, falling blissfully asleep, thoroughly sated. Jada sunk into the euphoria, fully satisfied for the first time in a very long time.

8

Jada dreamed of Javier, of them together, and of him dominating her. These weren't nightmares, but dreams putting smiles on her face throughout the night.

In the morning, the alarm rang and Jada tried moving. Her pussy was aching. It had been used, so cruelly, and she knew it would be awhile before it was accustomed to the level of activity she began to suspect would be the norm.

Javier got up and used the bathroom first. He told Jada when he came out, "Don't start the shower yet, we have a couple things to do first."

Jada stopped and looked at him. "Boy, we ain't fucking again this morning. My pussy hurt."

Javier laughed. "Calm down, baby. Remember, I want to trim you down.

Jada opened her eyes wider and then looked down at her pubic hairs nestled between her legs. "Oh, I forgot daddy. Sorry."

She answered the call of nature and then opened the door, longing for a bath or shower; hoping it would make her feel a bit less stiff. Jada wasn't used to so much cumming. Rather, she was glad she survived the evening.

Javier came in and said, "We'll get you the right stuff later, for now this should do."

He began filling the tub with water, checking to make sure it was the right temperature. "Hop in amor, and relax." He kissed her and Jada felt a tingle run down her body.

"Take care of your baby, Papi."

"I will don't worry."

Javier helped wash her in the tub, and it flushed out the results of last night's passion. It was strangely erotic, and somehow more than that, it was intimate without being heavily sexual. Javier soaped Jada gently and then rinse her down.

"Ok Mami, time to shave you." Javier told her. He started the water to drain from the tub and left the shower running. Javier opened the shaving gel and rubbed it on Jada's left leg, starting low and gently scraping away the faintest stubble.

He was gentle, and careful, and Jada wondered

how many women he had done this to. "You're not bad at this. You've done this before, I see."

"Yes, I was taught how." Javier said gently shaving her thigh.

Jada felt warmth spread through her as she felt Javier shave higher and higher. She licked her lips and watched him work. He started on her right leg after making sure the left was done, all except what she was nervous about.

Javier again moved gently, massaging as he shaved it, making sure not to cut her. His gentle stroke that was just perfect. After shaving Jada's legs, Javier began shaving her armpits to make sure she was perfect there, too. "You're too beautiful to be looking so primitive, my love." Javier then had Jada sit on the edge of the tub, and lean back.

"I'm going to trim it first, and then shave. I'll put you a small heart right here." Javier tapped his finger above her labia. "If anyone sees it, they'll know you're loved."

Jada couldn't say anything; her aches were a thing of the past, as she felt her desire increasing watching Javier.

He used scissors to trim the hair away and then electric trimmers to shape the heart he wanted. Jada tried to ignore the buzzing and vibrating that sent little electric shocks of pleasure through her. Then, he lathered her pussy with the shaving gel and began. Focused, Javier made sure his entire attention was her.

He carefully shaped the heart and moved the folds of her labia to make sure the area was smooth. Jada held in her moaning, sighing or whatever noises that were trying to come out. Javier was so gentle, so careful. It wasn't hard to remember this was the guy who had whipped her into a sexual frenzy last night.

Javier finished both labia, rubbing his fingers over it, making sure. "One quick rinse and you're all done, amor." Javier took the shower hose and rinsed, going over her legs and pussy several times. "There you go, how does that feel now?"

Jada rubbed her hands down there and was surprised how smooth her pussy was. "It's really sensitive, not painful though."

"I know, that's what the goal was, to make you sweet. This will increase your stimulations."

Jada's eyes popped open. "Oh shit! Are you telling me more?"

"You'll get used to it. You'll never want to have hairs again."

Javier lowered his head as if examining his work, and then by surprise gave Jada a lick around her clit area.

"Oh, stop. Oh, stop daddy," moaned Jada. "Aren't we about to go, God?"

"Si, amor."

"I don't have anything to wear. Can we go by my apartment?"

"No worries, all you'll need is something for today. We'll drive to Atlanta and pick up some outfits for this weekend. Next week, we can discuss your living arrangements." Javier told her stepping into the shower to see to his own needs. He washed himself in minutes while Jada looked into the mirror and saw her little dark haired heart sitting perfectly centered above her vaginal area. It was nice and kinky.

Meanwhile, Javier was shaving himself, much faster than he had with Jada. He finished quickly and got dressed. Reaching into the closet, he pulled out his luggage.

"You're already packed, I see?"

"Yeah, from last weekend, I never unpacked."

Jada thought about last weekend and how things had changed ever since.

9

---

*J*ada and Javier grabbed some burgers and fries from Grindhouse and then stopped by Jada's apartment. Javier waited while she changed and then helped her pack. Jada tried packing more things but Javier shook his head "no". They loaded the bags in his car and got some lattes from Starbucks on the way. His Subaru was spacious although a little weird to Jada. She pictured this best-selling author to be driving a SUV but knew he wasn't as flashy as other Papis. Javier during the drive began filling Jada in on what to expect, and what to do when at the "Ranch."

"A couple named Jimmy and his wife, Sarah run the joint. Jimmy, his brother Alex, and I were best buddies in college. When we were on campus, we discovered how much money was in this line of work.

Jimmy's father passed away right after we graduated and left the family ranch to the boys." Javier merged north onto I-75 and continued.

"The family started off raising crops but had trees growing so they invested in them. Different pines and oaks but then the demand shifted to paper. At that time, I was living in an apartment in Athens, trying to finish my first book while having watered down soup for dinner every night. James called me and said he had an idea, and wanted to talk about it."

They continued north and Javier glanced at the dashboard and continued his story. "His mother and father had taken out a few insurance policies, and Jimmy had invested the family fortune in CD's mainly and some other stocks. They wound up buying the largest farm area in the county along with other busi-nesses. That also came with some issues with the IRS which the brothers just settled recently. In order to deal with those tax fuckers, Jimmy and Alex sold most of the plots surrounding the ranch, but still had acres left. They calculated the costs, including some up closer to Atlanta that their grandfather had won by luck in a poker match. Unfortunately, they only had about a little less than three million dollars once they sold everything."

"Why would they sell the land up near Atlanta? They could have just rented or leased it. They'd be good right now?"

"That is what I told Jimmy, but they said they needed cash to make the dream a reality. Meanwhile, his brother Alex was in New York and visited the Bar D ranch, and raved about it. He told Jimmy he wanted one here in Georgia, to serve the Southeast and wanted me to help. I told him I was so broke if it took a quarter to go around the world, I couldn't afford it."

Jada smiled. "I know that feeling."

"Yeah, well. Alex told me his idea, to make a ranch here to attract the rich and shameless, but he wanted something more, something like a big ass family. He wanted bondage but not the sadist shit. Bar D wasn't kinky enough for him." Javier held Jada's hand while continuing to drive. "So we talked and I helped them work out ideas. I minored in Engineering, and gave them so things on logistics. We designed the ranch to be renovated; practically destroying it to make a new one. We then had a series of small guest bungalows built; each room enough for ten to fifteen people. Jimmy and Alex just finished having the construction done on a larger one that can hold up to one hundred. While we were in the construction phase, we realized there would be some problems. The more we thought about it, the more we realized that we needed more space. We concentrated on building the ranch first then letting people know by word of mouth.

Jada thought about that for a moment and replied, "Ok, you need customers, but you couldn't let them know you're here. Wow, that's tough." "How did you get so big, then?" Jada asked staring at Javier's crouch causing him to laugh. "Hey, you know what I meant, boy."

"Honestly, it wasn't me; it was Alex who dealt with that. He kept saying the answer was simple. Go to the strip clubs in Atlanta, and introduce yourself to a couple people, kick it with them, and then tell them about this new ranch about ninety minutes away which will be hosting these lewd weekend getaways. Hire some beautiful women to wait on them, and they'll be back. Keep the fees low, and raise them over time to keep it "exclusive".

"And apparently it worked."

"Not really, we ended up with a few patrons. After my first book was done, I was trying to get it published. I was in New York and talking to my editor and who would become my publisher, and told him about this project I wanted to be a success for my friend. My editor said it was kinky shit, and it would ruin my author career, so leave it alone. Later, after he left the room, a woman overheard our conversation and asked me about the ranch. She said she was a submissive, and wanted to know how to contact this place, so she and her husband could go down there for a weekend?"

Jada laughed. "How convenient!"

"Yeah, they arrived and spent the weekend, and gave us feedback on what was missing such as product demonstrations, classes, and tutorials on how to improve techniques. She also gathered information from the New York ranch, and suggested we start an annual competition, break out into the scene, so to speak. We talked it over with them and decided on having the pony races."

"Ok."

"Crazily, it worked. People from Atlanta that were going to New York in the winter, now come here to have a good time," said Javier. "We have representatives from the sex toy manufacturers and suppliers come once or twice a year, and spread the word about Circle B to their clients."

"How many are members now?"

"I honestly don't know. It's in the hundreds though. Jimmy and Alex have been quietly buying back the surrounding lands as the money and property becomes available. We need this to be exclusive, and most people who are into this can't swing the thirty-five grand a year membership, plus of course, any incidentals."

"Thirty five thousand dollars a year, for a weekend strip club?

"Yep, the price is intended to keep the less serious out, and others will keep their mouths shut before spilling the beans." Javier told Jada now entering the city limits of Atlanta. "To that, you'll have to sign a NDA when we arrive."

"Ok, so I sign swearing I'll have my eyes put out if I ever breathe a word of this to anyone? You could have told me when you were spilling the beans?" Jada chuckled.

"Well, my love. The moment I first laid eyes on you, I knew I could trust you. "Did I tell you I love you?"

"No, but I do, too. We're in this heavy kind of early but you did take long enough to let me in."

"You weren't ready, and I owe your best friend and mother a great deal. They did what I could never do, by opening the door to the cage you have been living in."

"I was thinking about that yesterday afternoon. When I was in high school, I enjoyed being bound by my ex. I had no idea it could be as hard as it was yesterday, last night, you know." Jada said blushing.

"It only gets better, more satisfaction, as your experience grows," Javier said smiling as he took the Buckhead exit.

"More satisfaction? Javier, I thought my pussy was going to be torn apart. I don't know if I can handle anymore of you."

"Don't worry, you'll handle it, and in time, you'll be begging for it. Trust me; I won't let anything bad happen to you." Javier said rubbing her hand.

They pulled off the highway and into a shopping area. Javier pulled into a small parking area and then drove around back to a secluded area. He got out and took Jada's hand and walked to a building, inside an unmarked glass door. Jada looked around seeing it was a clothing shop that specialized in suggestive clothing for men and women.

Javier waved at the clerk and she came over. "Hello, Darlene. I'm glad you're here. This is Jada and she needs something to wear for the weekend. You know a full kit."

"I was wondering what you were doing here." "You know Jimmy. He's still faxing in those orders even though we got smartphones now."

"I told him to get an iPhone. The man is stuck in the 80s."

Jada looked confused and Javier whispered, "Darlene's one of our first members. She runs the shop. Usually if you want something, you mention it to Jimmy, who faxes Darlene. Her husband, Danny will bring it, a day or two later."

"Not this weekend, I've got work to do and can't go play." Darlene said pouting. "I have to work or I won't be able to go watch next week's."

Javier laughed. "So help us out, a girl who 's out on her first weekend, what's in now?"

Darlene started showing Jada outfits, and Javier would nod or suggest that perhaps later it would be better. He picked out a couple of tennis skirts, and matching sports bras. He also bought Jada a dress that would leave almost nothing covered, a leather mini-skirt and bustier blouse. With Darlene's help, Jada watched Darlene and Javier discuss her wardrobe and turn to her for approval. Jada felt uncomfortable and almost asked if they intended to find someone else's clothes when Darlene spoke.

"This woman's a good submissive, Javier. She hasn't smacked you yet. She's so ahead of schedule." Darlene said looking at Jada. "She's gorgeous from head to toe. God, I wish I was going to be there this weekend."

Jada blushed, and looked at Javier finding him smiling back. "Yeah, Jada's amazing. Last night was an awesome practice."

"Last night? How long have you been submissive, Jada?" Darlene asked.

"Well I was a bit in high school, but I haven't done anything ever since. We just started dating, so I guess you can call it that."

"Wait, it was your first time, not the high school thing?"

"Yeah, I'm a newbie," Jada said looking duped.

"Subspace, on your first try? Oh, Girl, you are going to be something with a little bit more training."

Jada and Javier chattered while Darlene bagged up everything. Javier paid and then drove off and stopped at another store a few blocks away with human models in the window. Javier bought himself a pair of shorts and a white polo shirt. At a third store, Javier bought Jada a small suitcase for her outfits.

After shopping, they went to a nearby diner for lunch. Jada wondered about the costs of everything. "I have a question, baby. Who pays for the membership?"

"A dom pays. Everything is a gift including the clothes. Otherwise, there wouldn't be any pleasure and we'd be called pimps."

"So, we will go to the ranch, and spend the weekend playing master and slave, or dom and sub?"

"Si and you'll enjoy yourself by finding a satisfaction you never knew existed."

"What if you're wrong? What happens then?"

"We leave, as soon as you want. Our safe word is 'Red' and ends play immediately. Absolutely, no hesitation is tolerated when a safe word is used. If you say red, take me home, we'll leave immediately."

"Wouldn't that be a problem for you? I mean wouldn't your friends say something about our sudden departure?"

"They would be concerned, and curious, but they wouldn't stop us. Don't worry about what others might think. They don't have negative thoughts. The purpose of this ranch is simple, Jada; enjoyment."

A waitress came and Javier paid and they left. They headed back to the city going south.

Jada tried quieting herself, but she felt stress building. Could she trust Javier to respect the safe word? She needed to prove he would stop and back away when it was used.

The car approached an exit on the far right and Javier signaled a turn on a two-lane road at the end of the exit ramp. Javier had just completed the turn when Jada said, "Javier, red, the safe word, red." Javier hit the brake hard and pulled to the road's shoulder. Once the car stopped, he put the transmission in park and then turned to Jada.

"Jada, what's wrong, are you OK?"

"Sorry, I just needed to verify that this 'red" word works." Jada admitted embarrassingly.

"Ok. I'm glad you waited until we were away from traffic." He leaned over and put his arm around Jada. "I understand your worries, Jada. I'm not Carlos, and we have no one like Carlos as a member."

"I know baby, I was just testing you. I didn't mean to scare you."

Javier told her it was OK and asked if it was okay to start driving again. Jada gave him the thumbs-up and he pulled off.

10

————

They passed through a small town, and fifteen minutes later, Jada gulped as Javier turned into a small two-lane drive with a small sign on the corner that read *'Circle B – No Trespassing'*.

Javier turned and drove past. The road extended and a large guard shack stood ahead near an open gate. A man in an NFL team jersey waited in the middle of the road holding a clipboard. Javier slowed down next to him and rolled down the window.

"Good afternoon sir and welcome back."

"Good afternoon, Tim. This is Jada. I'll check her in at the main house." Javier said handing over his driver's license and cell phone. Turning to Jada, he said, "Please give the young man your ID and cell phone."

"Thank you sir, and madam. Enjoy your stays."

"Thanks, Tim."

Javier drove away and said, "The ranch is 900 acres or so. Mostly woodland, which gives us a good cover. You'll see it's marked no trespassing and hunting along the perimeter. Also, here there are many security cameras, facing outward and inward, along with motion sensors planted in case someone trespasses. Those caught are arrested immediately and fined."

They followed another curve in the road and reached a nearly empty parking lot. Javier parked while another man with a cart approached them as Javier and Jada got out. "Eddie, what are you doing here?"

"Sir and Madam, I'd be happy to see to your things." The old man had a black shirt with its red collar and tie flipped upwards.

"What in the world did you do to get punished?"

"I said something bad to Mistress Destiny, and she ordered one weekend of the red collar.

Javier sighed and handed over three bags that were in the trunk. The man attached tags and wrote on them.

"Edward, allow me to introduce Jada, who's going to experience her first weekend. Is Mistress Destiny here this weekend?".

"Nice to meet you, Jada. Sir, I haven't yet seen her around, but I know she'll be here."

"Thanks, Eddie. Let me show Jada around before we head in."

They walked towards the main house and Javier explained. "Violations of the rules will result in punishment. Since you're my guest, I'd be the one deciding, and to prevent any mistakes, I've decided to get you a pink collar, which means novice. If Mistress Destiny is going to be around, she is a zealot for proper respect and deferential treatment."

Javier went on to tell Jada to remain silent as often as possible, don't gape or gawk at anyone. Act like you belong, and act normal. Everyone here is living out a fantasy including her.

Javier and Jada entered the main lobby, and turned right where they spotted a man wearing a Braves jersey behind a counter. He smiled extending his hand when they approached.

"Javier, nice to see you again. We missed you last weekend."

"Hi, James, this is Jada. I'll need you to set her up with a kit. Sorry about last weekend I had something come up literally at the very last minute."

"Doug said something like that," said James. "Jada, welcome to the Circle B, since you're with Javier, I know he'll go over everything with you. What kind of banding would you like this weekend?"

Jada looked at Javier confused.

"Jada is new, I mean very new. She's been through

the basics, so I think a pink collar would do just right. Later, we can set up the full kit and box."

Jada was confused as James left and came back with a clipboard and pink nylon collar.

"Here you go. Here's a short questionnaire, Jada and this NDA. Here's your collar." Javier, would you put it on?"

"Certainly! Collar position, Jada."

Jada went down quickly to her knees, keeping her thighs straight and reaching. Her hair was brought up behind her neck along with her hands. She remembered at the last second to look downward. Javier placed the collar on her neck, not too tightly. Jada was then told to rise.

"I think black for me would be about right this weekend," said Javier. He looked over the papers on the clipboard and handed it to Jada. "Fill this out, and the next time you come, they'll have everything for you."

Jada took the clipboard, seeing it had basic questions; name, address, age, sex, sexual preference, and medical information. She skimmed at the section where it mentioned the amount that would be forfeited if she violated the agreement. It did have an exception for law enforcement in the investigation of any criminal activity.

"Senor Javier, you missed my race last weekend." A voice said from behind Jada. Jada looked back to see the same woman from the pony video; Slave Monica.

"Ok, Monica, I know you won. Doug couldn't stop talking about it," said Javier playfully while embracing her.

Jada looked at Monica and saw the woman was a little taller than in the video. She was dark skinned and had shoulder length hair sparkling in the light. Her arm muscles were on full show even though she was wearing street clothes.

"Monica, this is Jada."

Jada held out her hand and shook Monica's. "Nice to meet you. I've heard a lot of good things about you."

"Sorry, but I hadn't heard anything about you yet, sweetie. If you're the reason why Papi here missed my race, then you owe me one," Monica said in a friendly sarcastic tone. "Hi James, since Leo isn't going to be here, perhaps blue would work this weekend."

James returned the greeting and stepped away for a moment. A few seconds later, he returned and handed Monica a collar. Jada noticed Javier was putting on his black leather wrist band.

Monica put her collar almost simultaneously. "God, I just don't feel right without one of these anymore." Once it was attached, Monica sighed. In a submissive way, she spoke. "Thank you, James for giving me my medicine."

"You're very much welcome."

"With your permission sir, I'd like to offer Eddie my assistance," asked Monica.

"Certainly, I was about to suggest you go check on him."

Monica bowed and quickly headed for the exit. Jada was unsure what she had just seen. Returning to her clipboard, she marked off she had no medical conditions that required treatment, nor did she take any regular medications, no allergies, and, etc. Finally, she finished filling out the papers, and signed the agreement.

"Here you go, sir," said Jada, adding the 'sir' after a moment of uncertainty.

James took it smiling and said, "It's all right. The elders consider the collaring to be the moment each become submissive. It's no longer required to be as selfish as society demands of us. We'd never expect such from a pink collar." He glanced over the sheet. "Looks okay. Welcome to the Circle B, Jada. Here's the submissives' newsletter, and the rules of our establishment." James handed over two more sheets and wished them well.

Jada read over the rules which were essentially what Javier had told her. Rule one; safe, sane and consensual is our code; safe words will be respected always. She read through the rest and then looked over the second sheet.

The newsletter "Subspace Gazette" announced that ten participants from the submissives would have the honor of representing the Circle B family at the Annual Memorial Day Pony races, and hoped everyone would support their efforts. It also mentioned the upcoming collaring ceremony of Master Walter and Submissive Cindy, and wished them the very best in happiness.

There will also be a submissive swimwear contest on the pool deck next Saturday, and the winner would get a private exhibition with Mistress Destiny.

Finally, the newsletter mentioned that Rimjob the Cat had blessed the ranch with a group of kittens. Whoever interested in taking one, contact Mistress Destiny.

Jada giggled wondering if everyone here was insane. When Javier finished talking to James, he said, "If you're ready Jada, we can walk around a bit."

Jada nodded and slightly bowed. "Yes, sir."

Javier took her leash and tucked it into her pocket. He then gestured for her to go on his right.

"The largest residence has suites and the public scene areas. The suites are on the second and third floor. The dining room is through there, and the public scene areas are all to the left here. In the back, there's a pool and pathway to the lodges and the race track."

Javier opened the door and escorted Jada through the pool deck. "Sarah's supposed to be back here. She's the owner Jimmy's wife and slave. She was collared here ten years ago and has re-collared with him every year since. The collar colors are explained in the rule book but I'll tell you briefly what they are.

- Blue: willing to scene, unlikely to participate in sexual intercourse.
- Green: willing to scene, including sexual intercourse
- Black: partnered, restricted scene opportunity
- Pink: novice, limited scene availability.
- Red: punishment, no scene possible.

Jada listened, and remembered that Monica had chosen blue, which meant she was willing to play, but not have sex.

"The colors are an easy means of communication; each member has a full set of colors, at the check-in counter back there. Some will switch, which is to say they are submissive at times, and dominant at times. Edward, who you met in the parking lot, is a switch. He spends most weekends as a submissive, but on a few nights, he will be dominant."

Jada looked at the people around the pool; clad women almost universally wearing collars, and almost half of them were green. There rest were wearing black or blue.

They walked down to the lawn and Javier explained further. "We have Tai Chi here in the mornings while helps with the grace and balance. If there's a collaring ceremony, which I understand there will be, it'll be held here-weather permitting."

"The Collaring Ceremony, what is that like?"

Javier answered. "It's the making of the dom-sub relationship official. Most are part-time with no strings attached. Sometimes, a dom will have more than one submissive. We call them harems. Mistress Destiny, who you heard of, is one of those who have harems."

"A woman has male slaves?" Jada snickered at the thought.

"A few do. When Destiny arrives, she'll probably have two or three with her. She has males I'm aware of, but also females."

"Straight baller! I think I like her already."

Jada and Javier laughed as they went down to the track. "This is what we call a one-fifth race track. The races are usually only one lap, but occasionally we'll hold some that are two. It's rare, maybe once a year at the end of the season."

Jada followed Javier back to the house as they

passed by the lodging areas. "Jada, these are where the most brilliant sessions take place. There are six areas. There's a board which show which are reserved right near the check-in counter. There are three reserved already, meaning that three can set aside for one night each. The public scenes are just that, public. There's no penetration, nor intercourse. However, there will be flogging, bondage, service, and even teasing, but no intercourse. If you want more, the members reserve the lodges. The understood agreement among us is that if you attend, you wish to participate, even if it's with a single partner you are with. Do you understand?"

"Yeah, I think."

Jada stopped walking outside of one of the lodges and said, "So this is an orgy room, and if you walk in, you have to participate. You don't go in just looking. You can limit participation to a single individual, but participation is expected." Jada turned back to look at Javier. "This is the most weirdest shit I have ever heard of. You said three were reserved, which means there will be three orgies going on tonight at least. Lord, I don't believe it."

"Believe it. One of the conditions you agreed to when you arrived here is to provide within one week a full screening for STD's. You also agree to provide the results every three months. I'll take you to the doctor on Monday, and like the rest of us, you'll provide James with a copy next weekend."

Jada's jaw dropped, even though testing everyone was good. "So anyone who's a member can check out my test results?"

"No, Jimmy keeps them in a safe, for the time until they expire. If you don't have a current test on file, then you can get buy by wearing pink, or red, depending on the mood James is in. The test is intended to keep us all safe, and I usually do mine every two months."

"I'm not an orgy kind of girl you know." Suddenly, Jada started feeling bad, which didn't make sense. She and Javier had fucking around for close to a week really. She walked towards a bench and sat, biting her lip, while trying to control herself.

Javier watched for a moment, then walked over and sat next to her. "Jada, it's not what you think. It's not Rome or anything like that. Remember the colors of the banding. Blue means you will scene, but not intercourse, black means you are with someone, and have limited scene opportunity."

Jada looked at him while taking his hand in hers and leaned in. "Javier, did you see how many people by the pool were wearing green, which means 'bang the crap out of me' doesn't it?"

"No, it doesn't. What it means is intercourse is possible only." Javier tried not to snicker. "After these scenes, the atmospheres are powerful, and sometimes the willingness to say no isn't always as strong as you might want it to be. The color system means we minimize the next-morning regrets. It reduces the incidents of someone saying, 'Oh my God, what did I do? I slept with him or her?' We all understand and respect that. If your usual partner isn't here, most times you won't wear the more liberal color; you'll put something on that signals you're kinda off limits."

"Then why did Monica say someone wasn't here, so she had better get blue?"

"Leo's her usual partner. He is a dom who has that kind of relationship with her. They aren't exactly a couple even though she spends most of her time in submission to him."

"Ok, so if I wasn't here, what color would you wear?"

"Whatever was appropriate. I swear—I don't know honestly."

"You're not answering my question. What color would you be wearing? Better yet, what color were you wearing before I got here?"

Javier looked at Jada for a moment and then looked off in the distance. He didn't answer right away as Monica was coming down the trail pulling a luggage cart with a half dozen suit cases on it. "There's Monica, we were just talking about you." Javier raised his hand. "Monica, do you have a moment?"

Monica stopped the cart and held it one-handed. Bowing her head, she replied, "Yes sir, how can I help?"

"Jada was curious about the color system. Please allow her to assist you with the luggage, and answer any questions she might have." Javier said as he rose up.

"Jada, go with Monica and return to the main house when you're ready, I need to talk to Jimmy for a few minutes."

Jada was confused. "So, you're sending me away again. Ok, fine. We got some talking to do when I get back," Jada whispered in Javier's ear before leaving. She stood up to follow Monica. Monica turned her head to look at Javier who shrugged. "Hey sweetie, what about the colors has got you in a bind?"

"I asked Javier what color he would be wearing if I wasn't here." They had arrived at a lodge and Jada grabbed a bag to help carry it in. "He said you were wearing blue because someone wasn't here. He wouldn't answer my question, and then passed me off to you."

Monica stopped unloading bags and looked at Jada. "Jada, when did you meet Javier?"

Jada said "I met him about seven months ago. I interviewed for a job, and I know this sounds corny, but I swear I fell in love with him—instantly." Jada wasn't sure why she had tossed in that last part.

Monica set the bags down and stepped to Jada. "Congratulations, Jada, he loves you, too." Monica then released Jada and picked up the bags again. "He quit wearing anything but black for the most part. Sometimes, he wore blue when we were short of doms but only did the public scenes."

"Why didn't he tell me that?"

Monica turned back and looked. "He's a dom with a dom's soul. Dom's don't answer questions on this subject to anyone ever. Especially to subs. Besides, if Javier had told you that, would you have believed him?"

"I guess not."

"Jada, Javier's a wonderful guy. We all knew he was in love when he started wearing black, only putting blue on when there was a shortage. We didn't know anything about you, sweetie, but he has changed since let's say around, Thanksgiving." Monica put the bags down. "Come with me. I'll give you all the dirt on everyone."

Jada followed Monica and listened. "Ok, but shouldn't I check in with Javier first?"

Monica seemed to consider but answered, "It's OK, he knows you're with me, and besides, if you upset him, perhaps you'll get lucky and spanked." Monica had a wicked look on her face.

Jada sighed and said, "That would be something, wouldn't it?"

They made a couple more trips, and Monica told Jada about the people they saw, and a few they didn't. Master Python got his name because of his twelve inches. Jada gaped at that one and Monica said it was absolutely true. Mistress Linda is a bit of a bitch; stay on your best behavior around her. Destiny is a stickler for Friday night deference, follow the lead of the other subs, and learn how to do things.

"Monica, how am I supposed to refer to everyone? I mean the other subs, and the other doms?"

"Call the doms; sir or ma'am. You can also call the women; mistresses without any problems. I usually call them by their title when opening conversation. For example, if I was trying to talk to Javier in a group I would say something like 'Master Javier' and then switch to sir for every answer I gave." Monica smiled. "It's not that confusing, just flow with it and you'll enjoy yourself. In time, you'll be dancing on the chains with the rest of us."

"Dancing on the chains?"

"That's what we call it when we have an orgasm from the scenes. Usually we're bound, you'll see, and the orgasm makes you shake the chains." Monica shook her head. "There's nothing like an S.H.O?

"What's that?"

"Submissive Headspace Orgasm. I'm going to beg

Andre' when I see him to do it to me. Shit, I could use a good workout."

"Girl, you crazy!"

"This place will take you there, believe me when I tell you."

Jada wasn't used to discussing sex or orgasms with anyone outside her mother and best friend, Britany. She was obviously uncomfortable and Monica noticed. "Jada, I have good vibes about you. You're submissive at heart and I also know you're an amazing especially if Javier already loves you. He's a great guy and a caring dom. Relax, go along with it, and you'll be flying in no time."

Jada considered, the word "flying", that's how she felt when Javier was whipping her ass last night. Flying along in her mind, it was the most incredible feeling she had ever experienced. The orgasms that came were intense, making Jada feel like she would rip her heart out.

The two talked a little more as they took the next load of bags into the main guest house and down to a section, Monica called the "sub rooms". When Jada returned, she saw Javier in the lobby talking to Doug.

"Gotta run Monica. There's my dom, man or whatever."

"Have fun, girl and please relax. Ok?"

"Alright."

Jada approached Javier and hesitated suddenly. Should she greet her Master or should she just approach head-down submissively? Let it flow Monica said, just approach and see what he tells you to do.

She came up to Javier and stopped a couple steps away, holding her head down.

"Jada, come forward. Did you enjoy talking with Monica?"

"Yes sir, thank you. She explained a lot."

"I'm glad, Jada, perhaps you should greet an old friend of mine, Master Doug."

Jada turned towards Javier's friend, hoping she was about to do this right. She dropped to her knees as gracefully as she could, bowing while placing her head on the backs of her hands before his shoe. She waited like Javier had told her to as she trembled in humiliation and suspense.

"She's wonderful, Javier. I saw her submissiveness last weekend." Doug said praising Jada.

"Excellent, Jada. You may rise."

Jada rose feeling more relieved than good that she had just been praised by another dom.

Javier placed his arm around her and said "Good girl."

At first, Jada didn't like that "good girl piece." She thought it was racist or sexist but for some reason, it gave her a bit of a rush. She felt like a kid again taking her gold star homework assignment home to Mommy after school.

Doug leaned in to Jada and whispered, "Jada, that was great. I know it's not easy, but you are doing great." He smiled and continued, "Just follow Javier's lead; you'll be a happy camper."

Jada blushed and looked down, hiding her face while turning slightly towards Javier.

Javier shook Doug's hand. "Doug, I think we should get changed, and then come down to mingle in a bit."

Jada walked on Javier's right and followed him up the stairs to the suites.

11

———

"Monica told me if I was late, you might spank me." Jada couldn't help but chuckle but Javier looked a bit puzzled by what she said.

"Relax amor, there are semi-private rooms for that." Javier said. "Trust me, the safe word here is inviolable. Any time you feel panicked or just need to break a scene, say 'red' and the game ends. Red means no play, which is why the punishment bands are red. No play, no way comes instantly when red has been thrown. If you're gagged, a stuffed animal is put into your hand, a ribbon is usually attached, to put around your fingers, to make sure you didn't drop by accident. Before that animal hit's the ground you are being released from the bindings. Then, you are comforted, cuddled and loved in a different way."

Jada shook her head and followed Javier to the room. She tried to relax and interpret what she was being told but it was too much of a stretch of imagination.

Once in the room, Jada used the bathroom and then found Javier had laid the suitcases out. He had some clothing set aside, and Jada saw her luggage open, revealing the clothing she had watched him pick out.

Jada asked Javier the question she was probably most afraid of. "What would you have me wear tonight, sir?"

"I think the white leather bustier, skirt, and heels would set off the pink collar nicely, don't you think?"

Jada smiled slightly. The outfit Javier had bought her was tiny, helluva skimpy. The skirt would barely cover Jada's ass, and the bustier would just barely cover her nipples, cut so as to allow most of her breasts to be visible. There were straps which would help hold it in place, but they were skimpy thin. The shoes which he had picked out had four-inch heels.

Jada nodded and started to grab the items her dom had selected.

Javier handed her a delicate silk thong he had picked out. Jada took them to the bathroom to try and squeeze herself into it. When she was finished, there was a two inch gap between the bottom of the bustier and the top of the skirt. The skirt didn't leave much of her assets to the imagination, and the panties he had handed her were thinner than paper. While not quite see through, they only shadowed her pussy. Worse, her newly shaven area was incredibly sensitive. Each step moved the panties over her labia, and Jada could feel each tickle now from its bareness.

When Jada came out, she caught her breath. Her dom was wearing a white peasant shirt made of expensive Egyptian cotton along with a pullover laced from the bottom of his ribcage to his neckline. The laces were loose. He matched it with dark gray pants and black leather motorcycle boots. His leather wristband was visible and hair had been pulled back to a pony tail held by a leather string. Javier looked wonderful, and if Jada had fantasized about this minute, she would have picked out something exactly like this for him to wear. She watched him buckle his belt; a black leather workman style belt.

Jada stood for a moment unsure what to do next. Javier looked at her and waved her over. Jada came and Javier leaned down to kiss her.

"You look lovely, Jada, absolutely stunning," Javier said beaming. "I bet you have several people lusting after you before dinner is over."

Jada didn't know if this was a good thing or bad. She just went along with the scene.

Yet, she blushed slightly and felt a thrill. She knew

she looked like a horny little slut and was getting horny. It definitely wasn't hard to believe when you consider how much sex they had last night. She had still felt a little sore from them, but she thought it wouldn't be a bad idea to jump him here and now.

Javier kissed her some more, and caressed her breast, fingering the exposed flesh, and giving the rest a playful squeeze. Jada felt her juices start churning and her stomach tightened.

Javier stepped back and rubbing a thumb along Jada's cheek, smiled and said, "God, you're so beautiful. A real queen."

Jada was nearly panting already, and replied with a mere, "Thank you." She was waiting for Javier to undress her and jump her before they left. But she was disappointed when he turned and pocketed her pink leash.

"Come on, let's go down and mingle with the others, shall we?"

Jada tried holding in her feelings of disappointment. Sighing, she followed Javier out of the room and saw others in the hallway. A blond woman about 5' 6" and fairly trim was walking holding two leashes. A male wearing a mask and a woman walked behind her, led by the leashes.

"Javier Darling, how are you? I missed you last weekend, I hope nothing unpleasant happened."

"Hi Linda, nothing major, just a last minute change in plans. This is Jada, and this is her first weekend with us." Javier said introducing Jada, "Jada, this is Mistress Linda."

Jada looked to Javier for what to do. How was she supposed to greet Linda?

"Hi, Jada, welcome. Javier you know "B" and I have a new toy, too. This is Janice, and while it's her first time, I felt Green would put her in the proper frame of mind."

Javier frowned slightly, and said, "Were you heading down? Jada and I were going for some frozen yogurt before dinner."

"Yes, we were. I wanted to reserve a scene space. I'll head over to a bungalow later, but wanted to introduce Janice to everyone first."

Jada looked around seeing, "B" was wearing hot leather pants, which appeared way too tight for any guy, and a criss-cross harness. His collar was a wide black. Janice had on some soft teddy fabric lingerie which meshed with her green collar. She looked scared, nearly shaking. Jada felt a bit exposed, but Janice looked pathetic and appeared as though at any moment she would pass out.

Javier took Jada by the arm and walked her down the hallway turning to the stairs while Linda took the elevator. Halfway down the stairs, Javier stopped.

"Good, don't greet anyone unless I tell you to. I'm okay with Linda, but we have a long disagreement about how novices should be brought in. The pink collar's here for a reason, and I think putting that girl in green was foolish."

"Did you see Janice; it looked like she was going to faint at any moment?

"I did, and you just relax, leave the rest to me, OK?" Javier said taking her arm and moving down the stairs. "I don't know what can be done. I'll watch. Let's see if we can ease Janice away from her, before Janice is sent home screaming to the police."

"Can't you do something about Linda? Get her to ease up a bit?"

Javier stopped and glanced around. "No, the unwritten rule is that we respect the dom-sub relationship. If we don't have to like what two people are doing, we do respect their right to do it. Consent is what matters. Janice is trying to be that girl, but needs a softer dom to start with. Don't worry about it, just follow my lead, stay near me, and if I invite you to visit with some other subs, they will be more experienced, and helpful?"

"Like Monica, right?" Jada asked.

"Yes, just like her. In fact, she would be a great mentor for you." Javier said escorting Jada to the café and taking a seat at a table with Doug.

"Jada, hasn't met Michelle, has she? Jada this is Michelle. She's a very good friend of mine, and I hope will agree to allow me to collar her one day." Doug said.

Michelle shook Jada's hand and Jada noticed that both of them were wearing green bands, which Jada now understood to mean that they intended to couple, probably with each other. Greetings were exchanged and Jada took a position similar to Michelle on the arm of the chair Javier was sitting on. Javier placed his hand on Jada's hip and it felt a bit possessive, but good. Jada listened to the conversation, a who's here kind of thing, and looked around. Doms were seated, and subs were either parked on the arm of the chair, or kneeling beside their partners. Some were on smaller tables along the wall, and a few doms sat alone watching.

Jada saw Monica along the wall and smiled. Monica was wearing a tight fitting one piece romper in flashing silver. The woman sharing the table with Monica was wearing what seemed to be latex top and bottom. It was very shiny whatever the material was. Jada realized that her outfit was more normal than most here. The Doms were more dressed, while the subs wore less. Some subs were leashed and others weren't.

Javier's hand gave Jada a small squeeze and she turned her head to find him smiling. Jada was smiling too, enjoying herself.

"Jada, will you do me a favor?" Javier asked.

"Yes, sir."

The man over there wearing the white shirt and black leather vest, you see him?"

"Yes, Master."

"Please go to him and say, 'Master Randy, if you please, Master Javier would like to speak to you if it's convenient.' and then go visit Monica and let her introduce you to Heather and the rest of the subs over there, OK?"

"Yes, Master." Jada rose to follow his instructions.

Jada approached the man in the leather vest and when he turned to her, she gave him the message. He thanked her, and she turned to go to the table Monica was sitting at.

Monica smiled and said, "Hey Jada, I was just telling Heather here that you are the one who appears to have captured Javier."

Heather laughed and welcomed Jada to the table. Monica rose to get everyone yogurt, and Heather said "Wow, that's a great outfit you got on, girl. You look outstanding."

"Thanks, yours is too. It seems like it fits you to a tee."

"Latex is like that, you should try it. So what do you think of the Circle B so far?"

"It's cool, so much fun for the weekend. Reminds

me of a country club of hedonism." Jada said with a slight smile.

"Yeah, hedonism run amok, with just enough rules to keep it civilized." Heather said as Monica returned with the cups.

Jada took a scoop, and almost jumped when Heather gasped.

"Thank God, I was afraid he wouldn't show this weekend." Heather said as she practically leapt to her feet. "Be back in a bit girls." She dashed off across the room to a man who had just come in.

Jada watched as Heather knelt and bowed to the man, placing her hands under her head before his shoe. Jada couldn't hear the conversation but the man nodded and his lips moved a little looking down at Heather. Heather responded by picking her head up and moving forward and placing it on his shoe.

"Cool, Heather is going to play with Andre this weekend. I'm kinda glad," said Monica.

"That's Andre? I thought you wanted him?"

"I do, we all do, he's the best whip dom around. He can do things with a whip that no one else can."

"I met a dom named Linda upstairs. She had a girl with her who was so scared she was about to wet herself."

"Yeah, Linda tends to push a little too hard for my tastes, but the subs know the safe word and the rule, so they are safer than they may feel."

Another girl joined them as Heather returned to grab her yogurt. She interrupted Jada and Monica's conversation. "Andre'll play this weekend; I'm going to hang with him for a bit, OK? Nice to meet you, Jada. Hey Nicky, I hope to take you on later this weekend." Heather said in a rush and then hurried back to Andre.

"I'm Nicky, and that was Heather hoping for a good whipping later."

Jada introduced herself and appraised Nicky who was wearing almost transparent miniskirt with black panels running from the neck to the crotch. Nicky was obviously wearing nothing under it. No panty or thong strings, nor was a bra strap. The outfit clung to her almost like skin, setting off her green collar nicely.

"So this is the Jada that has had the place buzzing all day." Nicky said to Monica looking at Jada. "I'm joking really. Word is that Javier brought his love has streaked through this place. Welcome, girl." Nicky saw the uncomfortable look on Jada's face.

"It's OK, what did Heather mean about taking you on later? Or is it indiscrete to ask?" Jada asked as she picked up her cup.

"Nothing much is indiscrete here, Jada." Nicky grinned wickedly. "I am the current deep throat champion, mainly because I knew Python before I came here."

Jada almost spit out her yogurt all over as she gasped.

Monica and Nicky laughed as Jada tried to control herself and swallow the rest of the yogurt. She wiped her mouth then fanned herself. "Sorry, you're the champion of what again?"

"Deep throat, you know, sucking a guy all the way down?"

"That's what I thought you said. Do we compete on everything around here?"

"No, it's not on the books. Python called me that when he brought me here, and the nickname has kind of stuck. He and I date outside of here, on and off again kind of thing." Nicky said grinning. "Don't worry. We all do what we want here. Monica is a racing legend."

"I know. Javier's told me, and showed me." Jada admitted.

"Oh, you saw the video of the practice race last year. That was fun," said Monica.

Javier arrived and put a hand to Jada's shoulder. "Girls, I'm going to steal Jada away now, if you'll excuse me."

Nicky and Monica said, "Yes sir" in unison. Jada rose and walked with Javier towards the dining room.

"I saw you nearly spit your yogurt out across the room and figured you might want to be rescued."

"Nicky introduced herself and I wasn't ready for

that." Jada said. "Let's just say it was a little Python over the top."

Javier laughed. "Yeah, Nicky is a bit of a wild card."

"Why is she so serious about her unofficial title?"

"Oh yeah. The Dom Python trained her before bringing her here," said Javier as they walked to the buffet line in the dining room.

"That girl Heather said she was going to take Nicky on, does that mean compete? Lord, how do you do that?"

"Heather will win; I think Nicky's double-jointed."

Jada stopped moving and stood there staring at Javier in line. "You mean they're going to compete as to who can suck the most dick?"

Javier turned to Jada and placed some food on her plate. "Yes, but they'll probably use dildo's or something in one of the lodges. There will be a crowd as the girls demonstrate their techniques. It's all in fun, Jada. They enjoy doing it or they wouldn't do it. No one makes anyone do anything around here, you know that."

They took their plates to the table and Jada sat beside Javier. She wasn't sure how she felt about a deep throat competition, or why someone would want that title. All she could do was shake her head at the thought of it.

As they ate, Javier started telling Jada about the food as Jada kept saying how good it was. "Jimmy hired a cook, and then as the memberships increased, hired a lead chef, but the restaurant wasn't ready to pay him what he was worth. Jimmy made him an offer he couldn't refuse.

Jada was facing the door and said to Javier. "I think someone arrived late." A large blond man in a silk black shirt, green wrist band, and black dress slacks strode inside.

Javier glanced over his shoulder and turned back."Python, he works on Friday's and tends to arrive around dinner time."

"Monica mentioned him, telling me he was called that because.." Jada stopped suddenly and blushed.

Javier smiled and said, "He does."

Jada put her hand over her mouth. "No, that's impossible. You can't be serious, 12 inches?"

"Measured, by more than one person, on more than one occasion."

"Damn, shame. That man would rip a girl apart. There isn't a woman alive who could take that."

"I know, he always wears green, and often sleeps alone because of that. Nicky's as close to a regular with him as they come, but even she takes time off. She isn't rushing to see him no time soon and no one else. I know she's hoping for someone else this weekend. Python knows the deal, and it's all good. Just a bit more than anyone could be expected to handle, at least on a regular basis."

Jada looked around and spotted Nicky with Monica. She also saw Nicky was intentionally ignoring Python. That monster would tear a girl in half.

As they finished eating, Jada noticed the subs seemed to be leaving the room. She looked around and noticed only a few were left, and turned to Javier. "Where did everyone go?"

Javier glanced up and said "Oh, you mean the subs. They went to the restroom. On this floor, it has a signs on it for Sub Males, and Sub Females. You might want to go and check it out. I doubt you'd believe me if I told you what they are doing right now."

Jada looked awkwardly at Javier, and then rose following a female she didn't know out of the room. Jada followed a woman, who seemed to be in her late 30's. She found the restrooms and walked into the Sub female room and saw women preparing themselves in more than one way. Along the counter, was a display of different enema kits. Jada realized what as going on and stopped dead in her tracks.

Turning, she found Monica smiling at her. Nicky was with her. "Hey Jada, please tell me you weren't using one of these as a water bottle," Monica said laughing with Nicki. "Relax sweetheart, it's not like that."

Jada looked at Nicky who was standing by the sinks checking her lipstick. "We tend to get nervous and a little, well locked up so to speak. This way we don't embarrass ourselves by dropping something during a scene later.

"Nothing ruins a scene like a Hershey bar dropping out," A woman, Jada hadn't talked to before said. Several of the women laughed and Jada felt humiliated and embarrassed.

"So, I'm supposed to do what--?" Jada asked.

"Did Javier tell you to do it?" asked Monica from the sinks.

"No, he said to go and find out for myself."

"Then don't, because it's your first night. I doubt that you'll get a lot of work tonight." Monica said as she stepped by. "But, it's a good idea in the future though, sweetie, especially if Javier decides to anal train you." Monica walked out the door and Jada stood there feeling like she had just been caught doing something terribly wrong.

Nicky stepped up and said "Don't sweat it, Jada. Can I call you, Jay?" Nicky got a nod in reply. "If Javier had told you we were all going to have an enema so we wouldn't shit ourselves dancing in the chains, what would you have said?"

"He said I wouldn't have believed him, and I don't know if I would have." Jada moved to the restroom stall and took care of her business. Her bowels had loosened by the shock of seeing this room and understanding its intent.

Jada washed up, checked her makeup, and

followed the stragglers out to find they all were headed to the lobby and then through to the scene area. The dining room was now empty while the waiters cleaned off the tables. Jada didn't see Javier anywhere, so she followed the crowd down the hallway. This part of the house was divided she realized. Some bigger rooms off the hall, some smaller, none with doors, and all had groups in them. Jada looked in at the first and didn't see anyone she knew. No Javier, Monica, Doug, or Jimmy. What she saw was a man in bindings smiling at a woman who was holding a cat-o-nine tail.

Jada went down the hallway and stopped when she spotted Javier in the second room to the right. The man she knew as Andre was holding a whip and Heather was in the chains. Jada stepped in and watched the scene, standing next to Javier.

"These people are straight freaks," Jada thought to herself.

Andre had bound and blindfolded Heather, and was working her lightly with **q**uick flicks of his wrist up and down her back. She was topless and had clamps on her nipples connected by a silver chain. She wasn't gagged but smiled hugely as Andre worked up and down her back, across her buttocks, which were still covered and down her legs.

Javier pulled her back and in a whisper with his lips next to her ears explained what was going on. "Andre is warming her up, getting her ready to enter subspace. Each time she jumps, her nipple chain tugs and increases Heather's pleasure, the pain and pleasure mix, mingle, and then the endorphins kick in and she'll fly soon."

Andre was flicking harder and faster now, his wrist spinning the whip now. It made a circle to the left and connected, then to the right, and connected again. Jada saw Heather, her eyes were glazed over, her lips were wet, and she was breathing deeply. Jada watched as Heather pulled at the chains binding her, her muscles tensing and relaxing as the pain moved, migrated, and became pleasure.

Twenty minutes of this had Heather panting now, and Jada thought that soon Heather would be having an orgasm, and she would see what dancing in the chains meant. It was so erotic, watching this woman get worked like that. Andre played her like a piano, hitting his notes perfectly. A hard swish now and then and the larger horsehair whip would whistle and then leave what Jada suspected was a stinging lash across whatever part of the anatomy Andre was focused on.

Jada became aware of someone behind her and turned her head to see Javier's head leaning to the side and Monica whispering in his ear. Javier's neutral expression became a frown and he turned to follow Monica out of the room and down the hall to the right.

Jada turned back to Heather and saw her grinding

her hips and moaning as each movement jiggled the chains connecting her nipples.

Jada turned and followed Javier, catching sight of him turning into another room down on the left. As Jada approached, she heard sounds of much louder swatting going on than Heather had been getting from Andre. She turned the corner and stopped. A man was suspended from the chains, wearing chaps and shirtless. He was sweating, gagged and holding something in his right hand. Two doms were behind him, a woman and a man. Both had large whips and were frowning as they took turns smacking the man hanging. Jada could see him jerk in pain, not pleasure and saw tears running down his cheeks.

She looked and found Javier to the left and went to him. Monica saw her and intercepted Jada by stepping in front of her. She whispered to Javier after he asked what was happening. "Carlos asked he be punished; he said he needed to be purged and didn't want a time limit. He also said he would end the play by dropping the safe word doll; that thing in his hand. We see he never entered subspace and is taking the pain. I'm a bit worried. Master Rick and Mistress June aren't happy either by the look on their faces."

Jada felt pity well up inside her and felt more people at the doorway enter silently. She looked at them and saw similar expressions of concern and pity on their faces. They didn't like this any more than Javier did she realized.

As she looked back she saw Carlos's hand twitch and then start to open. The doll started to drop and Javier entered her field of view, running towards Carlos and throwing himself between Rick's whip and Carlos's back.

Monica and several others all shouted, "Red red red." Many of them moved forward reaching for the bindings that held him.

Javier started holding Carlos and was soon joined by others who rushed to unbind him. Javier had been there before the doll hit the ground.

Jada moved closer, to hear what Javier was saying. She could just make it out. "It's OK, you did fine. You did wonderful." Javier kept saying over and over.

Someone removed the gag and Carlos wailed. "Oh God, she's dead, I didn't say good bye, I didn't tell her I loved her."

Mistress June and Javier took Carlos to the couch and sat him down. Rick on one side, June on the other, they kept hugging and talking to him.

Carlos calmed down after a couple of minutes, and looked up at Master Rick. "My mama, she was sick. I worked last weekend and didn't go to her. She died Sunday night, in her sleep, and I didn't say goodbye." Carlos's tears to pour again. "I thought this was more important. I thought I had more time and missed my chance to be with my mama." He buried his face into Rick's shirt and wept while others tried comforting him.

Jada stood there thinking, "What the fuck did I just see?"

She saw the doll on the ground and took two steps and bent down to pick it up. It was a figure of a cat with a ring attached.

Jada turned back and walked to Carlos, stepping as close as she could and held it out. "I think you've earned this." Jada didn't know what else to do believing he was crazy or something.

Carlos looked up and saw the toy animal. "Thanks." He reached out and took the animal and held it tightly. Jada stepped back and bumped into Jimmy standing behind there. "Oh I'm sorry, er I mean, I'm sorry, sir."

Jimmy nodded and whispered, "That was good, Jada."

Monica stood up and asked Jimmy, "Is Theodore around?"

"I've sent for him. He'll be here in a minute or two." James answered. "Is Carlos OK?"

Monica replied, "He hurts worse on the inside, that's why he didn't go to subspace."

Another man entered the room wearing a wristband and went directly to Carlos. He knelt before Carlos, others moving as he approached and began to talk to him. Javier rose and moved away, taking Jada's hand and pulling her with him.

"That's Theodore. He's a shrink, a real MD with degrees in psychiatry. He'll help Carlos tonight; he can do more than we can." Javier said to Jada. "Sorry, that's not the way a public scene is supposed to be, it's supposed to be about pleasure only."

Jada thought of Heather, and wondered if she had "danced in the chains" in the other room which she probably had. "I keep hearing that but is it true?"

"As far as Heather, believe me, she wasn't in pain, and by now, she's being cuddled after reaching sub drop," Javier said.

"Sub drop? Lord, have mercy. What is that?"

Monica who was nearby said, "Imagine being in the worst possible depression, coupled with horrible flu like symptoms. You don't want to move, can't get out of bed, and feel like you're going to die. That is sub drop; it's your body's reaction to the excessive amount of endorphins that are pumped through you. It will minimize or eliminate by cuddling and support."

Jada looked at her and said, "You've been in sub drop?"

"Yeah, and it hurts. You feel absolutely horrible. I almost quit the scene after my first. Javier helped me and brought me back."

Jada looked at Javier wondering if he actually fucked Monica. He quickly took her hand before the thought registered and walked her down the hallway. They turned a corner and he glanced back. Jada tried looking, but the wall was in the way. Javier turned left and into a smaller room. There was a love seat, with no other furniture. Just four connections on the ceiling, and a floor to hold down a sub.

Javier took Jada into his arms and kissed her deeply. "You're lovely, amor, absolutely beautiful. I've been wanting to bring you here all day. I've been day dreaming of this for months."

Jada kissed him back and snuggled into him. She really loved him despite all his crazy ass freakiness. Javier started to unbutton her bustier down. Once he did, it exposed Jada's breasts, and he slid it down her arms. Jada's breathing increased as he began fondling her. Javier reached into his pocket and pulled out a set of nipple clamps. "These aren't as extreme as the ones in the room; I thought these would do just right."

He rubbed her nipples causing them to erect. Then, Javier placed the clamp on her left breast, and then her right one telling Jada to breathe and relax into it. The chain between them dangled and swung with Jada's every motion. Javier took four black bindings from the shelf with small chains attached to them. Placing them on Jada's wrists, he connected them to the chains by the links that dangled at the ends. He then bound her ankles and chained Jada down.

Taking a black cloth from the shelf, Javier placed it

over her eyes and said, "This will intensify the feelings and make it easier to fall into subspace."

Jada almost panicked. Javier placed the doll into her hand and wound the ribbon through her fingers.

"You can stop this by saying, 'Red' or dropping the doll."

"Hey boy, don't kill me. I mean it."

"I won't, amor. Don't worry. Relax!"

onica nearby yelled, "Imagine being in the worst possible depressive state, coupled with flu-like symptoms. You don't want to move, can't get out of bed, and feel like you're going to die. That's sub drop; it's your body's reaction to the excessive amount of endorphins that are pumped through you. It will minimize or eliminate by cuddling and support."

Jada looked at her and said, "You've been in sub drop?"

"Yeah, and it hurts. You feel absolutely horrible. I almost quit the scene after my first. Javier helped me and brought me back."

Jada looked at Javier wondering if he actually fucked Monica. He quickly took her hand before the thought registered and walked her and down the hallway. They turned a corner and he glanced back. Jada tried looking, but the wall was in the way. Javier turned left again and into a smaller room than she saw before. There was a love seat and no other furniture. No tables, racks, or anything. Just the four connections on the ceiling, and floor to hold a sub.

Javier took Jada into his arms and kissed her deeply. "You're lovely, amor, absolutely beautiful. I've been wanting to bring you here all day. I've been day dreaming of this for months."

Jada kissed him back and snuggled into him. She really loved him despite all his crazy ass freakiness. Javier started to unbutton her bustier down. Once he did, it exposed Jada's breasts, and he slid it down her arms. Jada's breathing increased as he began fondling her. Javier reached into his pocket and pulled out a set of nipple clamps. "These aren't as extreme as the ones in the room; I thought these would do just right."

He rubbed her nipples causing them to erect. Then, Javier placed the clamp on her left breast, and then her right one telling Jada to breathe and relax into it. The chain between them dangled and swung with her every motion. Then, he took four black bindings from the shelf with small chains attached to them. Placing them on Jada's wrists, he connected them to the hanging chains by the snap links that dangled at the end of the chains. He then bound her ankles and chained her down.

Taking a black cloth from the shelf, Javier placed it over her eyes and said, "This will intensify the feelings and make it easier to fall into subspace."

Jada almost panicked. Javier placed the doll into her hand and wound the ribbon through her fingers.

"You can stop this by saying, 'Red' or dropping the doll."

Jada relaxed and forced herself to breath deeply the way Javier had taught her last night, was it only last night?

Javier started to caress her with a mink glove, and watched and Jada started to relax into the pain of the nipple clamps, and sensation of the mink glove. She started breathing more deeply, sighing as he caressed her legs, her thighs, and her stomach. It brushed the sensitive underside of her breast and jiggled the chain of her clamps.

The mink broke contact for a few seconds, and then was touching Jada's legs again, moving up them from the ankle, up to the knees and then continued up pushing her skirt up with it. The glove caressed her ass and Jada pushed back to the amazingly sensual feeling.

She couldn't see, she could only feel and hear, and Javier was silent, leaving feeling as her only sensation.

Jada felt all the touches were much more intense, and was surprised by the sudden flicking of something on her ass.

Javier began flicking Jada with a multi tailed flogger, gently and lightly, warming her up. The glove kept working up and down her caressing her where the crop wasn't, or had just been. Jada moaned again and began to grind gently whenever the glove was near her thighs. She extended her pelvis towards it, wanting more stimulation than she was getting there. Her labia was caressed by the silk thong, and she licked her lips and her panting increased. The whip fell across her ass and her thighs, up and down slowly, increasing in speed and in force over time.

The girl from Atlanta had lost track of time; flying on the cloud of subspace, floating on euphoria that mixed with arousal to make her compliant and feeling extremely good. Each sensation was more intense, more pain, with more pleasure.

Jada was getting close. She wiggled trying to get the glove to go there. When she did, her nipple chain bounced and waves danced down her body causing her to gasp. The whip blows became more frequent and harder and Jada jerked from the blows. Her jerking made the nipple clamps tug on her tighter sending her into a higher state of arousal.

Jada moaned as she neared cumming, and felt a hand pulling the clams from her nipples. As the blood rushed back into where it had been squeezed out of, the mink glove rubbed her breasts and it turned to pleasure as the whip struck her ass harder. Jada gasped as she was so close, one touch more might push her over the edge.

Lips touched hers, and hands caressed her breasts as the whip struck her again, Jada kissed passionately her tongue seeking its partner, and intertwining, dancing with it. A pinch on her nipples was all it took, and Jada cried out as she began cumming. She pulled at the chains, clenching all her muscles as she bucked in the effects. Her groin thrust outwards reflexively, and she expelled her breath in shuddering bursts as she rode the waves of pleasure that overcame her from. Her orgasm receded, and there was a buzzing in her ears, as the euphoria returned leaving her flying high from the endorphins.

Jada felt hands unbinding her wrists, and ankles, while also supporting her. She was carried, held in arms while a hand caressed her head. She realized she was sitting on someone's lap, and opening her eyes seeing she wasn't blindfolded.

Javier was smiling and whispering things to her. Jada could only focus on the words. "Amor, you did well, you were wonderful, absolutely wonderful."

Jada closed her eyes and sunk into his arms which were around her and holding her upper back. She could feel, not his hand, but a hand on her hip.

Opening her eyes again she realized her vision was a little out of focus. She turned her head and saw Monica smiling.

"Girl, you're a natural. I've never seen a first-timer dance in chains like that." Monica said standing up. She leaned in and kissed Jada on the mouth. Jada was surprised, and just as surprised to find her mouth responding back.

Jada turned to Javier. "There were more than two hands on me, I remember." Her memory was coming back slowly, dropping from subspace.

"Monica wanted to help, welcome you, and thank you for being so kind to Carlos."

Jada reflected for a moment and said, "I think I'm supposed to be mad."

Jada reflected for a moment and said, "I think I'm supposed to be mad."

Jada felt euphoric, erotic as hell, and yes, loved. There wasn't any anger. She looked up at Javier and said: "I do actually."

Monica caressed Jada's hair and said, "I'd love to stay, but I need to tackle Andre before he heads off with Heather. He's not going to deny me a workout I've earned." Monica turned and left the room leaving Javier and Jada behind.

"How are you feeling?"

"Good, really good." Jada answered. "I just need one thing."

"What's that babe?"

"I need you to take me upstairs, and do something else to me." Jada answered as she felt her pussy demanding attention. It literally was burning with desire, with need, and felt incredibly empty right now. The empty feeling would be sated by only one thing, Javier's dick shoved in her until she creamed all over it.

Javier helped her stand, and Jada found her legs shaky. She took her heels off to walk easier. As she did, she realized she was still topless. She looked around for her bustier and found it in Javier's hand.

"You can hand that right over here, sir."

Javier hugged Jada and held her close to him and helped steady her.

"If you don't get me upstairs now, I swear I'm going to find Python and pay him to jump on me."

Javier laughed and held her as they walked out of the room and back up the hallway. Jada looked into a couple of the rooms and they weren't in much use. Mostly people cuddled up in after scene play. They passed the room Heather had been in, and now Monica was in the chains. Andre was smiling as she responded to his attentions. Heather was sitting on the edge of the couch and obviously waiting to join in, to do for Monica what she had done for Jada.

Jada walked out of the public scene areas and across the lobby, her pace quickening the nearer she got to the stairs. The elevator arrived and someone

Javier knew but hadn't introduced her to stepped out and waved as he headed towards the back door. Jada headed for the elevator, and practically drug Javier inside. As the doors closed, Jada kissed him passionately. Her panties were soaked with pussy juices.

"Don't tease me, don't try to raise it, just do it." Jada said as the doors opened on the second floor.

Javier walked with her to their room and opened the door. Jada walked in and pulled her top off roughly turning to grab him. She fondled Javier's growing bulge and fumbled with his pants. Javier surprised her by grabbing her arms and holding them. He drug her to an armoire and opened it to reveal a collection of play toys.

"Fuck that shit, Papi. Give it to me raw. Don't play with me."

Javier looked surprised but complied. He went on to remove her skirt and panties were drawn off together causing them to drop to the ground. Jada stood nude. Javier then took Jada to the bedroom and brought her to the edge of the bed. He removed his clothes, pausing to kiss her as he revealed his dick before her. Jada's eyes focused on it, and she licked her lips. Javier had dropped the leash on the bed and began caressing her breasts while pinching her nipples.

"Get on top." Javier said which surprised Jada. She

never heard or read about a dom assuming the lower position. Yet, she didn't hesitate, moving until she was right in position. They adjusted until Jada felt Javier at her opening, and then she eased herself down, impaling herself on his eight inches. "God, yes, oh fuck that feels good."

Jada moaned as she rocked gently on him, full of his dick; her pussy stretched and feeling wonderful. She ground her clit into his pelvis, and her shaved labia was screaming with pleasure. She felt her cum building and she ground more *q*uickly, rocking and sliding on her Papi.

"Not yet, you don't get to come before your Dom." Javier said reading her signs expertly.

Jada bit her lip, and tried to slow down. Javier began thrusting upwards slightly, increasing Jada's stimulation, and bringing her orgasm even closer. "Oh God, please," Jada begged.

"No Jada, not yet, not until I give you permission." Javier said "If you come without permission you'll be punished."

Jada tried to slowing down more to suppress the stimulation. Javier moved his hand down over her clit. "Oh God, Javier, let me cum, please." Jada begged again.

"Is that how a sub asks for something?"

"Yes, this sub does, Papi."

Jada knew he couldn't deny her again. "Sir, Master, please let me cum before I explode on these sheets."

Javier grabbed her labia and pinched it; a finger reaching for and finding her clit at the same time. "Cum for me now, Jada. Cum for Papi."

Jada tensed when she started cumming. She bucked and Javier's dick slipped out as his cum came. He ejaculated on Jada's ass; streams splashing up onto her back. Her hands caught some and she pulled her hands around. Looking into Javier's eyes, she licked the splash of his cum off her hand. Her eyes sparkled as she licked and he licked with her.

There was a bit of yelling down the hall. Javier and Jada rose. As they listened closely behind the door, they heard the words, "Fbi, Hands up. Come out!"

"Shit! Oh my God!" Jada sighed.

They got dressed quickly as bangs struck their door.

"Javier Sosa. Come out!"

"We're coming out. Don't shoot us!" yelled Jada.

"Come out now."

Jada opened the door and there were FBI agents with guns drawn. "Come over here, Miss. Are you okay? That man's wanted for running a prostitution ring, trafficking, and solicitation."

"It's not me. I don't know what you're talking about. Don't believe them, Jada" yelled Javier.

Jada was ushered out and the agents went in and arrested Javier.

───────

Three months later, Jada was back home with her parents in good standing and now employed. She'd come in from work when she saw on the CNN that Javier Sosa, the famous writer, and those who were running the ranches across the US were convicted of all charges as well as unlawful sodomy. The reporters mentioned that the victims were groomed as young as sixteen and lucky to be alive. The report also named some former government officials and celebrities that were involved. Jada's mother was shocked sitting next to her daughter telling her I told you so and Jada hushed her. Only Jada and her mother knew what was going on while Jada's father and brother looked at the TV.

"Damn criminals," her father yelled.

Meanwhile, Jada wondered if CNN was telling the absolute truth.

"Damn, Papi almost got me," she told herself while her mother embraced her.